IN THE SHADOW OF GIANTS

By

Lazette Gifford

Copyright 2014 Lazette Gifford

An ACOA Publication

www.aconspiracyofauthors.com

In the far future, after humanity has spread across the stars, the Norse Gods ask a former companion's help, but Loki may not be ready for another round of Ragnarok.

In the Shadow of Giants
A Conspiracy of Authors Publication
www.aconspiracyofauthors.com
Copyright 2015, Lazette Gifford
ISBN: 978-1-936507-54-2
Cover Art Copyright 2015, Lazette Gifford
(Created with Carrara Pro 8, Photoshop CC)
Editing by: Chizzy Editing, Chizzypress@gmail.com

First Print Edition, June 2015

This novel is dedicated to my wonderful husband Russ, who never thought it odd to go out and buy yet more books and learn new things. And so we charged halfway across Minneapolis to buy books on the Norse and the Norse Gods (though I had brought several with me) and I sat in a hotel room for a couple days reading and taking notes and had a wonderful time. Thank you.

The stars knew not where their stations were.

Poetic Edda

Frigg sat at a table in an ice-white room devoid of any decoration -- because she made the room this way -- and felt the runes moving in her hands. She held her breath for a moment before she cast the ancient stones across the table, watching the future unfold. The paths tangled as ancient lies blossomed into new troubles and the future moved closer to chaos.

She could do nothing except to gather the runes and cast once more, hoping for change. She could see the fates of others, but she dared not reach out her hand and alter what would be. The runes gave her no hope, but Frigg wouldn't weep for those visions . . . not yet.

CHAPTER ONE

A myth never tells the entire story. . . .

Somewhere near the end of second shift, Station Time, Koil sensed a subtle change in the area beyond his office. He put aside his ink pen -- an old-fashioned regard he still held for things long outdated -- and closed the cloth-bound ledger where he had been totaling the day's profits. Torin would type the entries in later; Koil and computers did not always get along.

The impression of *wrongness* remained, like the touch of cold fingers brushing against the back of his neck. Koil stood, forcing himself to remain calm as he keyed open his office door. He stepped out into a small alcove beside the bar. A few patrons had gathered, drinking to celebrate the end of their dreary work day. Friendly people, and Koil nodded in passing, but the *wrongness* persisted, emanating from somewhere in the area beyond the genial and popular drinking establishment.

A dozen steps took Koil from the low-key bar and out into the overwhelming colors of *Chaos*, a thousand-square-foot of gambling den. Three tiers of metal, permaglass and plastic fanned upwards from the floor, giving the establishment almost twice as much floor space even with a large open area in the middle. As usual, every level held a myriad, moving vision of station personal and ship crews. Bright lights flashed in blues and greens, cascading across the walls and floors, while bells, music and laughter filled the area. The overwhelming input masked what he sought. Whatever brought the coldness into *Chaos* wasn't drawn because something unpleasant had happened here. Koil never let anyone lose too much at the games. However, *Chaos* gave the locals and visitors the gift of chance they lacked in the rest of their regimented station and ship lives.

He glanced up and down the tiers, noting a group of Chinese in their black and red uniforms leaving through the eastern door, holding to the symbolism that was a huge part of their lives. Locals thought it amusing when Koil named his four doors for directions from the old world, but they never noted how he rarely went in and out except by the north door.

One of the Chinese glanced his way and frowned. The group sensed him. They had something of a tie, he and the men of the *Imperial*. The Chinese were trouble and there had already been one questionable death among their crew. Koil wanted nothing to do with them, but they returned to *Chaos* in small groups every few hours. He didn't trust them. They carried the scent of Old Earth and he wondered what drew them here, so far from home.

They were not the problem he sensed lurking out in the crowd.

None of his people gave a sign of trouble. Torin smiled as he took the stairs to the second level where he'd take walk along the slot machines and video games, keeping people honest. Old-fashioned games, the locals had mocked at first . . . but they kept coming back.

All normal. Nothing out of place.

Then why had his mouth gone dry?

Something was not right. Koil stared across the flowing mass of people, letting the colors blur into spots of station personnel in blue and a plethora of other colors from the local workers and people passing through the station.   He let his senses open, searching for whatever had drawn his attention.

Koil found the disturbance almost immediately in the shape of moving shadows that had been lingering just outside of *Chaos*. He focused as the problem came through the wide north doors in front of him. The two tall men quite plainly didn't belong here and drew attention where they passed.   They radiated *otherness*; dark-haired, dark coats, and carrying enough electronic equipment to set off a few alarms as they crossed the threshold. They never slowed, their heads bowing in unison as they came towards him. Torin started down from the tier in a rush, but Koil waved him off. He knew these omens of another time.   Huginn and Muninn: he would have known them any where and in any form.

Odin couldn't be far away. Koil started towards the two, anger taking the place of the worry from moments before. *Not here*. Odin and his bastard followers were not welcome in *his* place. Even after so long, the old rage rose as though from fresh wounds of the body and soul, and a scar across the side of his face ached --

Distraction. He realized the Ravens were nothing more than an obvious distraction and he started to turn --

He found the two standing at his back, a place he would *never* trust them again. Dion and Roth were dressed in earth browns and ocean blues, no less regal or symbolic than what the Chinese had worn. Oh yes, he knew the names they used in this new age just as they no doubt knew he went by Koil. Their true names were too powerful, still laden with old magic, to use freely even in this new, wider reality. Besides, those names were also obvious, especially in a group traveling together in an unusual ship.

Koil had never traveled with them. He took a step away, already shaking his head --

And Roth, ever unwise, made the mistake of trying to grab

Koil by the arm.

Koil leapt out of reach, snarling with anger. "Don't even think it," he warned, his hand going to the dagger he wore as Dion put a hand on Roth's shoulder and held him back with such an insubstantial touch. Koil stood a few inches taller than Roth -- almost as tall as Dion himself -- and glared at Roth, mistrusting him more than Dion. "Get the hell out of my place."

"I told you this was waste of time." Roth's voice, as always too loud, drew attention from everyone nearby. Torin headed their way once more; no way to stop him this time. By now the boy knew what had walked in. He would be wise, Koil hoped.

"I want a few words with you, *Koil*," Dion said with a bow of his head, politeness covering something else. Dread? Worry? Koil used to be able to read all the Norse, but that had been a long, *long* time ago.

Not long enough.

Dion wore his blond hair longer, beard shorter and kept the eye patch rather than replacing his missing eye with something modern. Tall and regal, he made blocky Roth look like a thug, though perhaps the impression came more from Koil's feelings towards the man.

Koil shook his head with a growl of an answer and lifted a hand to stop Torin from coming any closer . . . and Roth grabbed his arm.

Every bit of tech equipment in the casino, and probably this part of the station, went crazy, despite his wards. Koil heard the wail of alarms like the sound of distant wolves as shouts of dismay rose all around. The Ravens' eyes narrowed as their left hands went to the comm equipment in their ears and their right reached for weapons.

Dion gave a signal to the Ravens. "Please escort Roth out of the establishment."

Roth cursed loudly, but one glance at Dion's face stilled

him, surprising Koil. He wouldn't have thought Dion still held such power over Roth, who clearly wasn't happy. Roth went with the Ravens, passing Torin without a glance, out to the station's wide hall beyond *Chaos* where the three stood like baleful ghosts staring in at civilization.

The electronics reset and machines rebooted with sluggish fitfulness while the lights in *Chaos*, and elsewhere on the station, stopped flickering. Koil got his temper in control as Station Control made a statement about a momentary glitch. There would be a lot of nervous people on the station for a few days.

"Is anything wrong, Koil?" Torin asked, in no better mood than Koil. He moved to stand beside Koil and stared at Dion.

Dion stared at Torin, his bright blue eye narrowed. He resembled an ancient Old World rogue with the eye patch, so out of place in this age of regen and replacement. There were reasons he dared not replace the eye and break the line of power, though. This was a man out of his time, but one who grasped a great deal more with one eye than others did with two eyes. Without a doubt, he saw the secrets in Torin.

"Everything is fine, Torin," Koil belatedly answered and patted the young man on the shoulder. Koil stood taller than Torin, though not by much. Thinner, darker Koil seemed more akin to the Ravens than to Dion.

Dion distracted him with the remembrance of things better left long behind, though he had always known this meeting would someday happen. They lived in cycles and the worm never let go of the tail to release the circle and set them free. Fate decreed they would cross paths again. He thought he'd prepared himself for the emotional shock, but the sight of Dion and Roth tore open old wounds.

Torin held his place, blue eyes narrowed and distrusting. Koil had told him about Dion, Roth and the others. He kept no secrets from the boy, but he didn't think Torin fully appreciated the danger of the moment.

"I have a ledger for you to copy, Torin," Koil said quietly. "Please go do the work now."

Torin stared at Koil, his face going red and perhaps both shocked and hurt, though he kept the emotions from his face. He looked prepared to argue, but he must have seen something in the face of the man who had raised him. There were times when a person didn't argue with Koil. Torin gave a curt nod and stalked away, back through the bar and into the office. Dion watched him go, contemplation in his face.

"Why are you here?" Koil demanded, taking control. He wanted this confrontation over with as quickly as he could manage.

Dion gave an elegant glance around the area, his right eyebrow raised in mock disbelief that Koil asked such a question *here*. Koil didn't move and Dion finally gave way, though he spoke with a touch of magic so others didn't hear, unsettling some equipment close by. Better a little electronic trouble than to go anywhere private with this man he could in no way trust.

"The Chinese have taken one of our own and they're upsetting the balance as they try to gain power," Dion explained with a slight twitch of his shoulders, as though he thought to shrug and stopped.

So, he'd been right to keep an eye on the Chinese and now wondered why they kept spending time at *Chaos*. Dion coming to him in this situation made less sense, though. More than simple mistrust kept the two apart; there had been too many lies, too many secrets and far too much treachery in the past.

"So they've taken one of *your* people. I should care because . . . ?" he asked.

"You should care for the old ties we share --"

Koil cut him short. "We share no such ties, not any longer." His voice had gone cold as endless winter. Dion blinked. Had he thought Koil would be so easy to manipulate? He barely held his rage at bay. "You've no right to try to use that old, lost call to try and drag me back into the mud."

"It is a life-long connection."

"You *died*. The link broke." Koil dared him to say otherwise. "I don't care what the hell happens to you, Roth, or the others."

"Let me put this to you in a more personal way." Dion leaned closer, seeming to grow in stature. "First, the Chinese are making a move directly against us and I have noticed they are trying to gain control of this area in particular. They are doing so because you, *old comrade*, have made the station a place of potent magic. You have created a powerful base and the magic calls us like bees to honey."

Koil hoped his surprise didn't show. He'd never considered the possibility, though he knew a flux grew here, belonging to him and a part of his nature. He hadn't considered how the power might feel to outsiders who had a link to him through old Earth and forgotten tales. "I still don't see why I should give a rat's ass if you and the Chinese go at each other."

"Think of this in terms of personal gain, Koil. You were always good at that." For a moment -- oh yes -- Koil saw the old fire as the blue eye narrowed in disgust. Dion leaned away again, perhaps rethinking his approach. "If the Chinese win in this area, you will be out of here."

"I'll rebuild somewhere else."

"Will you? Not if the Chinese continue to win. They have no place for chaos in their ranks, you know."

"Not here, perhaps. The universe is wide --"

In the moment he said those words, something moved on the edges of the human expansion, something ill-disposed towards anything from earth and grumbling at an old constraint, lately weakening.

Koil blinked and Dion nodded, knowing beyond a doubt what Koil had sensed in that moment. "There are reasons why humans neither pass Thiassi's Eyes nor venture beyond the

Hellewagen, though they never understand why. Something powerful sits there, sleeping but malevolent towards any intrusion. If the Chinese win, they plan to ally with this being they have designated as one of their own, winning power with the symbolism. If this works, they will destroy everything we are."

"I wasn't surprised to find you here," Koil admitted, drawing a confused look from Dion. "I knew you were in the area. I know every name the ship has taken and every world you've visited." Dion looked surprised. "I know the trouble you've caused, the wars you've started . . . and the name of every brothel Roth has been kicked out of. You need to rein your boy in, Odin."

"Roth -- *Thor* -- is none of your concern. All you need worry about is working with us in this time of trouble."

"And what if I say no?"

Dion's head tilted slightly to the side. "I'll have Thor kill the boy. I could sense his Aesir blood, you know. Did you really think you could hide the truth from me by sending him away?"

"I never tried to. Aesir blood, *not* Risi," he said and startled Dion yet again. "Torin is not *my* son, Dion. You're not paying attention: *I know every brothel Roth has been kicked out of.* If you tell him to kill the boy, I'll take great pleasure in telling him he killed his own son and you knew it. And he'll know the truth of those words, won't he?"

The future hung on this moment as Odin's face went hard and the old anger returned. Koil had known the inevitability of this moment: but what did they truly face this time? Was this the *Dusk of the Gods* or the *Doom of the Gods*? He couldn't tell. He didn't think Odin could, either.

The sounds around the room dulled and the colors muted. Koil had already been pulled away from the place and into a different path. He hated Odin for the loss of everything he had enjoyed and everything he'd built through the ages.

But if he had truly wanted to escape from this moment, he should never have built here and waited. This confrontation was his fault. He had stayed in a place where Dion, Roth and even the Chinese could find him.

Dion watched him, waiting with more patience than Koil expected. "Roth used to be a different man," Dion suddenly said. Unexpected words.

"And you know why he changed."

Dion glared, his anger so strong the room grew decidedly colder.

"Damn, the system must have a real glitch," someone nearby said. "Hell."

Dion blinked and the cold became more metaphysical than real. Plainly, he wasn't happy. And Koil enjoyed this part, reminding him so much of the old days when he would taunt those fine Aesir Gods who had pretended they ruled the world from their icy lands. Well, they were no different from any of the other ancient Gods from that strange, fabled world.

"Why would you raise Roth's son and obviously raise him well?" Dion asked at last.

"My own revenge," Koil answered. "Oh, not to kill him. No. Instead, I made him cultured, intelligent, urbane . . . everything Roth is not. I followed you like a whipped dog for centuries until I got my hands on a child. I can be patient. I also knew you would come here sooner or later. Our lives run in cycles and there is no escape -- but there can be change."

Dion didn't understand, but he wouldn't. Odin manipulated knowledge and never dealt with chaos incarnate. Koil owed the Aesir nothing . . . but damn, his curiosity would drag him into trouble anyway.

"Shall we have Roth kill his son -- *your grandson* -- or shall we try to be more civilized this time around and not kill *anyone's* children?"

Dion scowled. "That was a long time ago and a different place."

"Easy for you to say. You have your son with you. Where are my sons, Dion?"

"That was a long time ago," Dion repeated, the chill returning to the room.

"And you've plainly so changed, since the first thing you did is threaten to kill Torin." He lifted his hand and waved away whatever Dion had started to say this time. The *Alfater* never took well to being interrupted and his anger grew ever more chilly. "Shall we try to be more civilized this time around? We can discuss the trouble in my office over a glass of wine . . . or ale."

"And now, suddenly, you'll cooperate? Why?" Dion mistrusted the change.

"It's in my nature to be changeable," Koil replied, a truth Dion admitted with a nod. "It's also possible, being where I am and in contact with so many people, that I might actually have information which might help. Get your boy. We have things to discuss and I want Roth where I can see him."

Where he knew Roth couldn't go after Torin.

"You must trust us, my old friend."

Koil looked at the man. He would never trust Odin and his son, but even so, he took the two into his office.

CHAPTER TWO

Whispers.

A slow, languid twist, a movement of minutes or months.

Flexing essence.

A memory of otherness, long past.

Existence became reality, though not in the shape of a body as other beings knew such things. Awareness of *being* came with a thought. Consciousness began returning, a latent thought at a time, whispering down through the hours, weeks, months, years, centuries. No hurry. No need to rush.

Slowly, slowly . . . but at some point came awareness of confines circling him, a limitation and an annoyance. A shell. There had been a rock shell before, heavy and cumbersome. He had wanted to know what lay beyond the wall placed between him and elsewhere. He had cracked the shell and found nothing, so he created and created . . . and rested again.

Awakening now.

A sense of his creation still existing; changed, wondrous, dangerous, good and evil. What had he put forth?

His thoughts had become attuned to the thoughts of man though he had not created *them*. That had been another's work, later. He had been aware of humans during his long sleep, invading the places he had made for his Gods. Servants at first but they soon became willful creatures, those humans.

They had spread everywhere, to places he had not expected to find them, having gone so far away from the paradise world he'd created.

And they were *loud.* Nothing could sleep through their incessant noise and movement as they darted here and there, shouting to each other across the emptiness of space.

P'an Ku moved, flexed his essence again, pushing oh-so-slightly against the new shell, watching the surface bulge outward and return again. Not yet. Not quite yet.

But he was done resting.

CHAPTER THREE

The elegant room held a faint scent of jasmine while the light, ignoring the reality of modern fixtures, flickered as though they were candles in a soft breeze. Chu Jong bowed his head as he entered, giving an *almost* polite greeting to the venerable God who sat like a regent at the immaculate table. Tea waited, the cups perfectly arranged on the red lacquer surface; the ancient pot was made of *zi sha* clay from the Jiangsu province and a testament to an ancient past neither of them would welcome returned.

Chu Jong thought someone might be standing behind the three panes of the *pingfeng* but he barely glanced at the painting of an elegant crane and flowering cherry tree before he settled into the chair before the tea, silent and respectful.

Chu Jong and Di Jun did not get along these days. Di Jun cared too much for the disgusting humans. The power of his aberrant interest held the other Gods back from greatness as they dragged the humans along with them as though they were an ill-made anchor that could neither be lifted nor discarded as long as Di Jun held on so tightly.

What did the fool care? He was a God who made stars and played in the sky. Chu Jong had dealt with the humans from the start. A shame he hadn't let his son drown them all.

He spoke none of this aloud. There were other matters they must address, and what he felt about humans would not matter in this meeting.

They drank tea: a *keemun* blend: a touch of sweetness, a lingering memory of a world long behind them. Apparently, Di Jun wanted him to remember the past. Neither spoke. And then, finally. . . .

"I have remembered an old proverb of late, Chu Jong." Di Jun tilted his venerable head, the perfect vision of a white-bearded sage. Such a vision no doubt worked well at cowing humans. Di Jun had accepted too much of the human's view and lost his own way, never noticing when he left the true path of glory. "May I say such a thing to you?"

"Most certainly, old friend."

"*By a long journey we know a horse's strength; so length of days shows a man's heart.*"

"A wise saying," Chu Jong replied and bowed his head once more, this time to hide the quick snarl. He didn't need antiquated proverbs to run his life. "One which we should all take to heart."

"I have looked upon your heart, Chu Jong." Di Jun's hand moved, a subtle gesture of dislike, but clear to anyone who could read the signs. Formality disappeared as Di Jun leaned forward, a touch of anger showing in his ancient face, the mask of politeness gone. "You are leading us to places we should not go. What gives you the right to decide the future without council of others?"

"Knowledge," Chu Jong answered, equally without formality and with a dismissive wave of his hand, a sign of how he felt about those others who hid away in their little pieces of reality. "The rest of you have slept, Di Jun. The rest of you have ignored the signs."

"The signs?" he scoffed. "Have you found a sacred turtle? Have you read the *I Ching* and --"

"P'an Ku is awakening."

The man blinked . . . frowned, covering a heartbeat of

worry. "You cannot know."

"How is it you *can't* know?" Chu Jong demanded, his tone far from polite and the words biting. "Have you dwelled so long in Ti Yu that you forgot to look to Shen and the place where we belong? We are *not* human. We should not dim our inner light until we can no longer see beyond the walls of these human *things*."

"You speak too freely. You have lost your way *and* your manners," Di Jun replied, his eyes narrowed and his anger close to the surface. "*Modesty is attended with profit; arrogance brings on destruction.*"

Chu Jong bowed his head to the pretentious recitation of another old proverb.

He pulled the dagger from within his robe and drove the blade straight through Di Jon's heart.

Di Jon slumped inelegantly against his chair, dead before he could speak another useless aphorism. A heartbeat later, the body began to glow, the light so bright Chu Jong shielded his eyes as he rose and stepped away in haste. He didn't leave until the body of the God had disappeared.

When he walked out of the room, the changeable hall of the great ship, the *Imperial*, held a hint of frantic red tracing through the walls as the others realized what had happened. He saw insubstantial figures moving ahead of him in a fog as cold came to the ship. Chu Jong wondered if any of the others would dare make a move against him now. They were fools if they didn't realize what was happening and he walked with the dagger in his hand to be safe.

Red Coat waited at the curve of the hall. Not a surprise to see him since chaos and death suited the monster. Chu Jong did not slow -- no, not even when Monkey King raced howling through the hall to stand with Red Coat. An infelicitous combination of bad traits between those two, but they said nothing as he went past.

He had set the universe in a new direction with a sudden curve towards perfection. Chu Jong made certain that when everything settled he -- and those who stood with him -- would be in control. He had created his own destiny, but he would watch for daggers everywhere.

The walls shifted in hue from a majestic blue to lighter green and finally to the color and consistency of ice as he neared the wooden door. He didn't knock; Chu Jong pushed the door open to a room with a blazing fire and a man seated at a crude table, writing out words in some ancient and equally crude language . . . a tale of power, lust and loss. The barbarian tried to rewrite the past with those intense and unsophisticated scribbles, as though he could change anything with words.

What this creature (Chu Jong would not consider this abomination a God) did hardly mattered and he would be rid of the fool as soon as he was certain it had no more use. The dagger still sat in his hand and how easy it would be -- but not yet. He put the dagger away. Soon everything would change; past and future lost behind the perfection of a new beginning. Chu Jong never said so to this fool since the writing kept him busy and they didn't interact, except at such times when Chu Jong needed what little information the barbarian could offer.

The figure scowled at the intrusion with no sense of pride and no manners. Chu Jong almost mimicked the reaction since the attitude hung so thick in the air. *No.* He would not succumb to such lowness. He bowed and the man smirked, as though a show of etiquette was something to despise.

"Is there some change you need to report?" the barbarian demanded and put aside his pen.

As though Chu Jong came here to report to someone in charge. Chu Jong frowned and his will overcame the power of the room so that the fire burnt low and a cold breeze ruffled the papers. The walls moved inward at his command; a none-too-subtle reminder to this fool of whose ship he travelled within.

This room could become a very small, cold cell if Chu Jong so wished it.

Baldr bowed his head, barely polite, but better. Chu Jong allowed the fire to warm again and the walls to slide away.

"I have killed Di Jon," Chu Jong announced without preamble. "There is now an empty place in the hierarchy and I will act within this chaos."

Baldr smiled, intrigued. "Did my . . . did Thor and the others arrive?"

"Oh yes." He almost smirked. This creature knew no fealty to his ancestors. Without such patterns, how could he hope for perfection? "And they went to Loki."

"They will draw him out where we could not," Baldr predicted with the slightest flicker of worry, the temperature dropping again.

"This remains to be seen. The plan has gone well so far." He'd had enough of the barbarian already. If he hadn't needed to keep a contact with him so he didn't slip the leash, Chu Jong would have as soon pulled the dagger and been done with this one as well.

Not yet. Baldr still had use. *If you are patient in one moment of anger, you will escape a hundred days of sorrow.*

"We will speak again later." Chu Jong gave a final bow of his head. He left the room with a steady step, though once outside he waved away the robes he wore and consigned them to atoms while he clothed himself in new silk. He always felt unclean when he left the barbarian.

Red Coat and Monkey King still skulked at the end of the hall; animals and barbarians, all of them.

CHAPTER FOUR

R oth and his two companions had returned by the time Koil started towards the office. Roth glared like a sullen teen, while the Ravens flanked him with impassive steadfastness. Koil had never been able to tell the difference between the two and he wondered if Odin could.

Koil's glare probably matched Roth's, but he had cause. He would rather have told Roth to go to hell -- and could have arranged the trip with his daughter, for whom hell was named. However, now wasn't the time to create useless trouble. He had sensed something in the moment when they touched on P'an Ku, and more than their old war was at stake now.

He ignored Roth at his back and led them to his private office, a place of real earth wood and subdued colors. Torin had taken the ledger and gone to his own room, so there was no confrontation at the door, at least. Another door led to Koil's personal rooms. He rarely wandered far from the gambling den. The Ravens crossed and opened the second door but did not go in, giving Dion a nod, both of them perfectly timed. Koil wondered how often they practiced.

Dion appeared impressed by the room. The wood alone, priceless in this place so far from where the trees had grown, was the envy of the few people who had gotten into his private retreat. The walls held the scent of home, a world hardly anyone on the station had ever visited. The room also held very little tech and was enveloped in extremely strong wards to keep whatever happened here safely inside the walls. There were more wards around the entire sector of the station he claimed as his own and they weren't there simply for his protection. Koil had a temper and sometimes he had to contain the power when his control slipped as it had earlier.

He signaled Roth and Dion to the leather chairs and he crossed to the little bar behind the desk. He did, in fact, keep ale there. Good ale, brewed on Earth and transported to the station at great expense. He could have magicked something similar, but the taste would not be the same. Hollow, empty of the real life that made this ale so rich.

He also had several goblets pushed into the far corner of a cabinet. He pulled them out: golden, ancient and more priceless than the walls and desk of this room. When he sat the three on the desk he saw even Roth's eyes go wide in shock. *Odin* and *Thor* had not seen those cups since last they all sat in Valhalla drinking toasts and insulting one another.

He poured the ale and another scent of earth filled the room. The Ravens moved to the door and guarded against intrusion. Odd how he felt better having them there, though they were the servants of Odin. They wouldn't let anyone in, which might be good. The Chinese had been to *Chaos*, after all, and they might be almost as much a problem as the Norse. The Chinese should not have come to him for any reason with their own God awakening, and now he mistrusted them all the more.

Koil settled in the high-backed chair behind the huge desk, mostly to make certain he had something solid between him and Roth. He nodded at the goblets and Dion took one and Roth did the same. No toasts, no boasts and no insults today.

"Eight days ago, a crewmember of the *Imperial* sent me a note saying he wanted a meeting," Koil reported, mostly because there was no use dragging the drama out. This was not a quiet drink with old friends, after all. "I knew the ship held some old Chinese Gods, of course. This isn't unusual. We had two of the Greek Gods through here last year. Eris and Hebe. Troublesome pair, really."

"The Greeks and the Romans were always too interested in their petty feuds," Dion replied, an amusing accusation from any one of the Norse. "Pretending to be the civilized Gods."

"They haven't learned any better. However, the Chinese are the problem now. I didn't know what the man wanted. I went to the bay to meet him, but learned he had lately died in an *accident*. I got out as fast as I could. What I didn't know was how this trouble involved the Norse as well."

"You weren't suspicious, even after one asked to talk to you?" Dion asked, setting aside the goblet. Roth did not, gulping half the contents. Koil poured him more, a small price if the liquor kept him quiet.

"I am the God of Chaos, Dion. More so now than ever. *Things happen.* Since the death, I have heard a rumor about P'an Ku is awakening. It took me some time to track down the reference. If he truly is awakening, we have trouble on our hands. He is the Chinese God of creation, who could -- and probably would -- wipe out everything if he doesn't find the universe pleasant when he awakes and looks around."

"Wipe out?" Roth repeated. He held tight to the goblet.

"Send us all to ground zero in a way that would make Ragnarok look tame," Dion answered before Koil could reply.

Koil nodded and sipped.

"You did nothing?" Roth demanded.

"Should I? We would go back to *chaos*. That would be good for me, wouldn't it?"

Roth started to snarl something, but Dion stopped him with a hand on his arm. "He's playing you, Thor. He loves civilization too well to want to go back to living in hovels with dirt packed floors -- and even those days would be a long time in coming. No, Loki isn't ready to give all this up."

"How do you know?" Roth demanded.

"Because he's talking to us."

Koil smiled.

Roth grunted agreement and drank. The light caught the golden rim and the reflection brought fire to Thor's eyes. Dion knew the game Koil played, who had a long grudge with his old friend Thor, the one who had betrayed him. Thor knew Koil would not have forgiven him. Koil -- *Loki* -- had wondered if Thor had changed after so many centuries, so many worlds. He hadn't, which made sitting here easier in some ways. He knew this Thor and despised him.

"So it's up to us," Dion replied, filling the emptiness as his fingers unconsciously caressed the goblet. Did he remember better days? Loki refused to think of those days before the betrayal. "The other Gods are scattered. Few of the pantheons have any cohesion the way the Norse do."

"And the Chinese," Koil added.

Dion nodded agreement. "They have focused on us for this reason. We are the only ones who have the ability to stand before the mass of the Chinese. In the power of believers, we might have the upper hand. They lost much of their hold before mankind left Earth. We managed to keep the myths alive a bit longer, at least, as humanity sailed a different sea and looked for guidance."

"Didn't you learn anything else?" Roth demanded leaning forward to strike the goblet hard on the surface of the desk. Koil gave him one cool, calm stare, which infuriated him more, as he expected. Roth glared. "What the hell good are you to us?"

"I can tell you that, despite a name change and a bit of magic, the ship remains in port here at the station."

Dion glanced at the Ravens. One bowed his head and left, running to find out the truth.

"Don't trust me?"

"*Never*," Dion replied.

Koil laughed. Lights brightened in the room and Roth looked all the more confused. Roth never truly understood. Thor had been, at one time at least, a favored God. A good God and well-loved. Things had changed for all of them and it hadn't been the *Twilight of the Gods* that caused the changes, either. There had been too much betrayal within Valhalla before the end came.

Dion watched Loki and waited; *Koil* wasn't certain what this apparition from the past really wanted from him. He had to be careful. If he were wise, he would tell the group to leave and never come back. If he were wise, he wouldn't have invited them into his office. If he were *truly* wise he wouldn't, as Dion pointed out, be talking to them.

He had never been mistaken for the God of Wisdom.

"I didn't know why they were sticking close to the station," Koil admitted. He sipped the ale and let some of his own anger drain away. He needed to think this through and ignore Roth, who represented a different problem from another age. "Now, knowing there are Norse involved, I'm not surprised. Whom do they have?"

Dion looked him in the face. "Frigg."

Koil's fingers tightened on the goblet and Roth didn't miss the reaction. Frigg: wife of Odin, mother of Baldr and Thor, and the one person in all his former life to whom Loki felt both a debt and even some gratitude. Dion knew it.

A test. *A true test.* He had not faced one in a long time and the thrill of anticipation swept through him.

Koil put aside the goblet. This needed a clear head. "They took Frigg because she has the power to see the fates of all people. They might well want such a power now as P'an Ku unsettles reality. They'll want to trace how their actions affect their futures and they'll want us to not be able to do the same."

Dion's face remained calm but the remaining Raven

straightened, a flicker of something uncomfortable crossing his face. Oh yes, always look elsewhere to judge Dion's true emotions. The loss of Frigg had to hurt his pride besides being someone he did, truly, love.

Koil would help Frigg. The thought surprised him since he'd intended to walk away from this game as soon as he got the information he wanted. They sat in silence, Koil pretending he considered the problem and Dion pretending he didn't know Koil had already decided. Roth drank more ale.

Sigyn came in through the door, moving like a thundercloud rolling over the station. Everything cooled in her presence as she glared at Dion and Roth. Dion must have given some signal to let her through because the Raven didn't try to stop her. Koil held up his hand, signaling her for calm, but he could tell she had no intention of stopping.

"What do *they* want here?" she demanded, a hand flung out in their direction. He was surprised lightning didn't flash from her fingertips and burn the two where they sat.

"We came to discuss a matter with Loki," Dion replied, shifting slightly in his chair as he looked at her. Surprised, *truly surprised*, to find her here.

"And why should we trust you? You tortured Loki, you murdered our sons -- and all for your petty myths. What lies are you telling now?" She moved to stand by Loki's chair, always by his side. She had made her own myths with her steadfastness, and she remained by his side although she had the right and the chance to move on. Why had the others not expected her to be here?

"You have no place here, woman!" Thor slammed his fist on the desk. "Why should we trust you? You're no better than he is, and worse probably --"

Loki had thought to say something in return, but he stopped when Sigyn leaned forward to stare into Roth's red face. "Tell me, Thor, where is Sif these days? Why isn't she loyal to you?"

No, Sif wasn't with Thor. They'd heard from her a couple times in the last hundred years. Sigyn knew the blade she used to cut at Thor's soul.

Roth almost came out of the chair and Dion's hand didn't look substantial enough to hold him back. Frost formed on the goblets and the light flickered, reminding Loki of days lit by fire and shadows he could never trust. He didn't want to return to such a time, so he put a hand on Sigyn's arm and gave her a little nod, a touch of a smile. She had made her point and he needed the calm to return.

Of course they had drawn more attention. Torin came to the door this time, anger etched around his bright blue eyes. The Raven held him back, but both Koil and Dion waved him in, and the Raven let the boy pass with a narrowing of his eyes, and a touch of his hand to his ear where he must have listened to other things.

Roth sat straighter, the glare back. "We don't let *his kind* into our councils."

Sigyn gave a contemptuous little snort and pulled a chair over to sit near the desk. Koil wanted to order her away, but they'd long gone past a time when she would do what he commanded without question. Besides, she might be wiser than him just now. She helped steady him as she had so often in the past, seeing him through the worst times.

"Get him out," Thor demanded, testing to see how far he had control. He was about to find out how totally unimportant he was if he kept this childishness up. "He's not one of us."

"I only have one eye and yet I've seen the truth about the boy," Dion said with a wave his hand. "Why are you so blind, Thor?"

Thor hated being rebuked, but he held his tongue, lifting a hand to Torin. Koil had been ready to move at the first sign of magic, but the hand dropped again. Thor gave Torin a snide snort of disgust and a toss of his head, so much like a bull in an arena that Koil felt a real temptation to create a flag of red cloth and send him chasing after it -- and perhaps add a couple banderillas to make the show more interesting.

Roth sat back, the glare returned. "Of course." His voice grew steady again. "What kind of monster are you, boy?"

"I don't know. What kind are you?" Torin asked with a snarl that almost matched Thor's.

The question confused Roth and surprised Dion. Had he thought Koil would keep the truth from the boy he raised? There were no lies between them. Koil knew how lies ate away at the good. Torin knew why Koil had taken him in and the truth about his father. He also knew what had started as an act of revenge had changed into something far better for both of them.

Roth liked none of this and seemed to realize he was the brunt of the joke, even if he didn't understand the jest. He growled words beneath his breath, his face growing darker, eyes narrowing with a flash of anger as he turned to Koil. They had not seen each other in a long time, and yet he realized Roth had held longer to the old angers. Koil hadn't forgotten. No, never forgotten or forgiven -- but he was cooler now.

He met Roth's look. "So tell me, is Baldr back with you?"

Roth's face went darker, a storm about to break in righteous fury, but Dion leaned forward. He felt ice in the air this time; he had touched a nerve for both of them. "You would be wise not to mention Baldr again," Dion warned, his voice as cold as a northern winter.

They stared, all three of them locked in a web of anger until Torin tapped Koil on the shoulder. "A delegation of five Chinese are here to see you."

That broke the old spell. "Are they indeed?" Koil pushed away from the desk. "Just me?"

"Yes. I'm not certain they know the others are here. I think they want you to go with them."

"Well, let's see where this leads, shall we?" Koil started for the door.

He wasn't certain Dion would let him go, or what he would do if Dion tried to stop him and the confrontation got out of hand. Roth made the first move, though, which didn't surprise him in the least. "What makes you think we'll let you --?"

Dion tapped Roth on the arm. "Sit down. Drink your very fine ale."

Roth threw himself into the chair, mumbling.

Sigyn took hold of Koil's arm and shook her head, face pale with worry, though she would say nothing before the other two.

"Watch the monitors. Keep track of what's happening." Koil bent to kiss her forehead, not caring what the others thought. They weren't worried about him but she was, knowing things were already out of hand. "They have Frigg, my love."

"They? The Chinese?" More worry followed her moment of surprise. "That's not good."

He agreed and gave a nod to the other rooms, waiting while Sigyn went into their private quarters. He trusted she would keep an eye on him and everything else.

"If I go, I expect you will follow," he said to Dion, knowing they would. He didn't want the two to think him so easily fooled. "Try not to cause trouble."

He walked out, Torin by his side. The younger man shook his head, dismay plain in his face once they left the presence of the others. At the corner of the alcove they paused for a brief moment.

"I don't like any of this," Torin admitted, but the glare turned towards the office and not to the Chinese.

"If it wasn't for Frigg, I would have booted the lot of them into *Asgard* and made certain the ship couldn't make port here for a long time," Koil replied, though he knew he didn't really mean those words. They had old ties he couldn't break. Or perhaps he didn't want to. Now wasn't the time to try and figure such personal problems out. "I'm going to talk to the Chinese and see what I can learn. The others will follow me. That's all right; at least I'll know where they are. Don't try to stop them, Torin. If I can throw the Norse at the Chinese, they can deal with each other."

"And they'll leave you out of this mess? Even I don't believe it."

He shrugged, but started away, Torin still by his side. "You shouldn't come with me."

"Sigyn will keep watch from here. She doesn't need me standing over her shoulder. And you've got enemies in front and behind."

"I might be forced to do something dangerous."

"I know."

He nodded. "Don't be obvious, then. I don't trust your father. Roth became duplicitous before Ragnarok. From all I can tell, he hasn't found where he misplaced his honor."

"I'll watch him." He glanced at the office door and frowned. "Why are they really here?"

"Old myths falling into place, I fear. *Axe-time, sword-time, shields are sundered . . . World time, wolf-time, ere the world falls.*"

"Only this is a different time," Torin said. "We'll control the myths."

Torin might believe so, but he hadn't experienced the older age and with those actions that still held them in their places, a thousand or more years later. Time had passed. Loki had died -- they all had -- and returned to travel the circle again. Change the legends? Koil feared control wouldn't be easy as he found himself pulled into this maelstrom of ancient myth and new disasters.

Or maybe he wanted to return to the old glory, the time before the lies began.

He hadn't believed P'an Ku was awakening. Koil had

thought the rumor nothing more than another of the many echoes of myths he'd heard through the ages, a whisper of disaster which always seemed to cling to the Norse, no matter what they did or how far they went from the old land. Maybe this new mess was their own fault for holding to ties of the old world, like the wood in the office or his ale from Earth. He had taken none of the rumors seriously until the Norse arrived, asking for his help: clearly this was a sign of the end of the world.

Too late to change old habits now. Koil crossed the casino to the eastern doors and gave a negligent nod of greeting to the Chinese. They no doubt took his attitude as insolence, but he was only distracted.

"My captain wishes to discuss with you such matters as may be important to us all." The man glanced towards Koil's office. Oh yes, the Chinese knew the others waited there.

"He should come and speak to me."

"No. The Captain does not leave the ship. There has been trouble in the past for those where he passes."

This might be the truth because some Gods simply could not turn off what they were. He had expected the answer anyway; few Gods would willingly come into his lair and he had thought Dion more than daring to do so.

The Chinese delegation waited for his answer, impatience plain on their collective faces. These were not people used to having to wait for anything. The group of five were some very minor Gods. The Chinese pantheon was overwhelmed with beings who were a mere step up from mortal. All of them acted as though they ruled the universe and Koil enjoyed the moment when a little of his chaos took them off-guard and two nearly fell. He acted as though he had not seen nor had anything to do with it.

"Let us go see your Captain, then," Loki said as though he had been considering the decision for some time. Never answer too quickly.

Koil went with the group out of *Chaos*, wishing he could have maneuvered them through the north door instead. No matter; he didn't lose much by going out their door. He drank in the feel of the place as he passed through the eastern door, walking out into the mundane world of a working space station. The halls outside of *Chaos* were dull grey and blue and he felt as though he stepped out into a foggy sky after the colors of his place. Sounds dulled and the feel of life receded behind the walls of metal and the careful shields he had made of magic.

Nervous people filled the halls, uneasy about the glitches caused during his initial meeting with the Norse. They'd get over their worries when everything went back to normal. He had no intention of letting this go too far.

Could he stop this very powerful Chinese God from awakening? Koil hadn't thought much about the real possibility before, but now he had to wonder why exactly the Chinese wanted him -- or any of the Norse Gods. They were not compatible groups. If Frigg would see the future while in their care, could a group so set in their ways act upon her visions?

People called greetings to him as he walked the halls. The friendliness surprised the Chinese delegation, who glanced at him with mistrust, as though having friends among the people he lived with was something evil. Ah, but they never left their ship unless they had to because they were *civilized* and the universe outside was filled with barbarians.

Those barbarians were more apt to remember the Norse God Loki than to be able to name any of them, for whatever good that might do. He was not remembered well.

Rage flared with the memories and the station almost suffered through another glitch. He caught himself in time. The faster he could get the Chinese away from the station, the better. The Norse, he figured, would follow the *Imperial* since Odin wanted Frigg back. If not for Frigg, in fact, Loki might have devised a way to boot both groups out into space -- and not into their ships, either. He wondered how long they would have taken for them to return to the cycle.

The Chinese didn't take the elevators to the docks. He wasn't certain if the Chinese passed on the usual form of transportation from a disdain of technology or if they didn't trust being somewhere dependent on modern power while walking with him. Wise, if the latter were the case. His moods had always been . . . well, chaotic. He wasn't certain he would have trusted one today either.

Taking the stairs made for a long walk down dully-lit staircases from one level to another. The light reminded him of twilight in another place. The farther they went, the fewer signs they found of people. These levels were mostly workshops and storage. The Norse, who without a doubt were behind him, had to hold back to avoid detection, though he doubted the Chinese were fooled anyway. Koil didn't hear so much as a stray footfall on the stairs. Sigyn watched over him, he knew. He smiled for her at one of the vidcams as they passed. She had access to all the station's vidcams, though station security didn't know it. She knew far more about tech than he did and worked well with it.

They left the stairwell and headed for the cold bays, and here, finally, they found more people again. He felt better for seeing them. The bay crews were a louder bunch, a bit more high-spirited and apt to shout from half a hall away when they spotted him. Oh yes, Koil had friends everywhere. He did not let anyone suffer too much loss in *Chaos* and they won often, too. He cheated no one.

"Look out!"

At Torin's shout, he ducked and threw himself to the right with his back to the wall, ready for treachery. The Chinese suddenly had company as several more of their black-and-red uniformed companions leapt out of a side hall, cutting him off from the Norse. He fought the first group, drawing a blade from the holster under his vest. The blade held enough magic to keep the weapon hidden from others and from sensors. The local humans were not in this area, subtle magic moving them away before the battle. Good. He didn't want them around for this kind of trouble.

His enemies drew in closer. He slapped the first group with a wave of magic and flattened three of the Chinese against the far wall. He didn't think they would get back up, however he hadn't expected them disappear in a godly glow. What was going on here? Did they die rather than be taken by the Norse?

More of the persistent enemy came at him. He couldn't use magic for much longer, though. The station's tech systems often reacted badly in the presence of magic. He didn't want to foul the station's systems, which could happen all too easily if he kept using the Old Powers. However, the Chinese were still coming, lines of them moving in on him and when he downed two, they simply disappeared -- not even a glow. A sound drew a quick glance to the side and he found the other Norse fighting as well. Where the hell were these Chinese coming from?

Torin attacked the enemy, scattering a dozen with a few well-placed kicks and a slash of his own knife rather than using magic. As the Chinese dispersed, Torin jogged to his side. Good boy. They had fought side-by-side before and Loki trusted him.

Power flared from the Norse and he flinched at the sight of so much magic let loose. Before he could speak, Odin ordered Thor to be more careful.

"Ha. We'll see if Roth listens," Loki mumbled. He kicked the man who leapt at them and almost took a cut in his own arm. He let Torin take the attacker, who promptly disappeared the same as the others.

"What the hell is this all about?" Torin demanded.

"More than either of us will understand," he replied with a grunt as he shoved the next one back. Persistent bastards. He could hear alarms going off on the station. Security had picked up on the trouble.

"We do not want to be caught here if the station guards come hunting," Torin warned. "We can fog the records and they won't know it's us, but only if no one sees us in person." Torin tapped his left shoulder. "Time to get serious?"

"Yeah. Or at least scare a few of them off."

Torin reached under the arm and drew a laser pistol. A very special one, with a practically-unending power source and a shield to keep it invisible to the station's sensors, just like the knife. Torin knew how to use the weapon well. He could fight with bladed weapons when he needed to, but Torin had been born to a different age. He was used to technology and used it well. He rarely worked through magic.

The sight of the laser pistol stopped another onward rush. Good. Loki hadn't been certain they would recognize the weapon. The Romans certainly hadn't last year, until Torin burnt Bacchus across the butt.

This group fled at the first sign of the weapon.

"What the hell was that all about?" Odin demanded as he stopped beside Loki.

"I have *no* clue, but I'm going to go find out." He shoved the knife into the sheath on his arm and started down the hall. Torin went with him, of course, the laser pistol back in the holster. Neither of them was happy with this behavior in their territory. Koil wasn't certain the Norse would come along. He really didn't want them to get more involved, but he soon heard the group following behind.

"Damn," he mumbled. Torin nodded and didn't look very happy either. Alarms continued to ring and this was going to be a mess to clear up with station management if he and Torin were caught in the midst of it.

Koil felt extensive and intrusive magic as he neared the bay where the Chinese ship sat at dock. Magical power overlaid the craft like a blanket and he wondered how they managed to make a connection to the technology of the station to get a berth here. He also knew the magic he felt was nothing compared to what they kept hidden inside the deceptively small shell. All the Gods who had taken to space had created such places where they warped reality to suit themselves.

Loki saw no humans in this bay. A small spell had sent them on their way when the ship docked. The Norse would have done the same. Neither group wanted the locals hanging around where they would sense something odd about the ship.

Loki -- *time to think in that name now* -- spotted the airlock door to their ship, bright red with the Imperial crest from another time emblazoned on it.

The magic in the bay hid something. Loki only realized the problem when he saw movement to his left and threw himself to the side and away, rolling out of the reach of --

Huge claws. Silver scales. The body should not have fit into the small, dark corner of the bay where it had waited.

Dragon.

Torin threw himself aside as well, though the dragon seemed intent only on Loki and he had to roll aside with no chance to get to his feet. The Chinese delegation that had led him to this trap had already passed through the lock without bothering to open the doors first. Koil scrambled away on hands and knees, hoping to get into the station's hall because he figured -- hoped -- the dragon would not go far from the ship.

Was the creature real? As real as anything else from myth and brought into shape. He hadn't the power to wish the dragon away, not against all the Chinese behind their magical walls who were now apparently wishing for the creature to destroy him. Dragon claws left a gouge in the floor plates where Loki had been a moment before. Scales crashed against tubes and conduits, sending a cascade of sparks, almost as pretty as magic, scattering across the room.

Loki backed away and got to his feet while the dragon moved forward, head low and watching him with unblinking silver eyes. Eastern Dragons were sinewy things, snake-like in many ways. He knew to watch the tail.

With a moment to think, he realized what he faced, his memory dredging up information he'd learned sometime in the far past. This was Tialong, the dragon who guarded the Imperial Palace and pulled the celestial chariot. Not a surprise, really, to find such a creature here. He probably symbolically pulled this new chariot, too. Tialong represented considerable age and power.

Loki backed away once more, but the tail moved and he had to leap aside. The head swung around, snapping at him, but he threw himself to the ground and rolled once more, avoiding claws as they tried to grab at him. The dragon, he thought, tested him to get a feel of the enemy. Maybe he surprised Tialong because he hadn't used any magic yet.

"We have no quarrel." Loki watched the neck curl as the dragon prepared to strike. Enemies everywhere except for Torin, whom he signaled to stay back. He had no intention of falling to this overgrown snake. He'd survived far worse from the Norse. He knew if he fell here he would return, but he wasn't ready to go into the long dark while his soul searched for the door back into being.

No, he wasn't ready to start over.

So he moved straight at the dragon, startling the creature, if nothing else. He drew the dagger into his hand, readying for the attack. He knew how to use the weapon. He had enemies and sometimes the humans thought he was a rich, easy target, but he'd managed to survive a long time and by more than luck.

He hadn't fought a dragon with nothing more than a dagger, though. The dragon's body tensed, and he knew the creature was about to make a serious attack. Loki leapt at the head, hoping to drive the dagger into an eye.

The creature proved too cagey and wise to let him get so easy a strike. The head swept to the side with a very snake-like hiss and he drove the dragger into the skin between scales on the neck instead. He flipped over the neck as he drew the dragger out, all in a half dozen heartbeats while the dragon's body convulsed once with the shock and the creature howled rather than hissed.

Dion and Roth with the Ravens were still close by. Roth looked smug -- right until Dion shoved him forward. "Help get it contained!" Dion ordered, though he wasn't long to follow into the battle, either.

It would never take the Norse long to join the fight. Roth, after a moment to curse, leapt in, drawing -- oh yes, drawing Mjolnir itself straight from their own ship and into his hand, the ancient hammer arriving with a sound as though a metal gong had been struck. The magic was going to cause more havoc on the station, but right now Loki didn't care. The dragon's head had twisted in an unexpected angle and caught hold of his arm, teeth cutting through skin and snapping the bone.

As the pain hit, Loki lost control.

Chaos in a docking bay isn't a good thing. The winds came first, as though they had a breach in the containment area. He heard alarms ringing and those, oddly, drew him away from the edge of madness. The wind died as his sanity returned and he found he had unsettled the dragon who had dropped him. He hadn't noticed; the fall hurt no worse than the pain of the bite.

Tialong howled in anger, the huge, gaping mouth reaching for him again.

Thor moved in between him and the creature, swinging the great hammer and hitting the dragon on the side of the face, knocking the beast back several feet where Tialong collided with a wall. The silver scales rang with the sound of a thousand small bells.

Thor glared at him. "Get the fuck up, Loki. I'm not going

to stand here hitting this thing all day."

Loki rolled to his side and moved to his knees, the dagger in hand still. Tialong's tail snaked around to get Roth, but Loki drove the dragger into the flesh between scales. He'd started to heal his arm, too, difficult though that was for a God. The powers had never been meant to help themselves, after all, but to serve others. He wondered if the rest of his former companions ever realized the truth.

Loki stumbled all the way to his feet. Though he couldn't use the arm yet, he leapt in to fight beside Thor. This was not a place he had ever imagined he would stand again. Ah, but he should have realized this would happen eventually. *Chaos.* He could never predict the future with any normality. Things changed when he was around.

Odin fought on the other side of Thor and the three of them forced the angry creature to retreat. He wasn't certain where the dragon would go, though he supposed that was no different than wondering where it came from.

Torin joined them. He moved to Loki's side, knowing better than to fire the laser pistol in the midst of so much magic, though Loki was about to suggest they find out how much chaos they would create. Torin held a long-bladed dagger and Thor gave Torin a look of mistrust, though he had no time for anything more. The dragon had pressed itself against the ship, ready to make a stand. Loki knew such a creature wouldn't be easy to take down. In fact, so far. . . .

"Tricking us," Loki said aloud and saw the dragon's head dip his way, eyes blinking. Oh yes, a creature of such ancient and powerful myths would have no trouble understanding words. "This is an old and wise dragon. He is giving way too easily."

Tialong tricked them with whatever game he played, but Loki couldn't see the pattern of what the dragon intended. What did the creature want? If he had been truly hurt, the others would have gotten him to safety. They would have --

Didn't need to open the airlock doors.

"Tialong is hiding something behind him! Get him away from the ship!"

They didn't need to because the dragon moved all on his own, a flowing both of the body and of magic. Behind him came a row of Imperial Chinese troops. And another row of them. And more --

Hell. What did they intend? To take over the damned station? He paused for a moment, but Thor did not. He leapt straight into the mass of soldiers. Maybe wise. Thor scattered their perfect symmetry and wasn't that what the Chinese Pantheon was all about these days? Perfect patterns. Everything in its place.

Which made Loki far more powerful than he had considered. Loki knew he had to be careful. Controlled chaos was not easy to create and hold, but he let the power spread out with a lift of his hand --

"Easy, Koil," Torin whispered nearby. He sounded a little breathless. "I hope to survive this."

Loki could have let go and chaos would have taken the Norse, the Chinese, the station -- ended the problem, at least for all of them.

But P'an Ku would still awaken. Damn.

Loki pulled the magic in and released a swirl of power cloaked in rainbow colors -- the rainbow had always been a Norse symbol -- and the unnatural cloud moved on a gust of wind, spreading in different directions. The dragon howled, perhaps confused for the first time in his very long life. The reaction also made him very dangerous. The dragon launched through the Chinese who had already started to scatter, and a few didn't survive.

Thor retreated in haste when Tialong tried to bite off his head. He got in a good swing sending the dragon backwards, but the creature surged forward once more and all four of them had to fight to survive.

Loki threw more chaotic colors into the face of the dragon, which worked as well as any weapon. The Chinese reformed in their perfect lines and rushed forward, weapons ready. Did they really think they could stand against the Gods? The mere numbers might be in their favor, so Loki brushed a few aside and once again they simply disappeared.

He hadn't used this much power in a long time, though. He had to stop. The feel of letting himself go was addictive, but he would be weak later. He threw a little more color at the dragon and sensed the arrival of the others before he saw them; the Chinese Gods had shown themselves at last. If they thought the Norse Gods had been beaten by their pet dragon and a few human soldiers, they were in for a surprise. Even Odin gave a contemptuous little snort.

The Chinese moved quickly, hands lifting with power. Loki couldn't tell if they wanted him or Odin. They seemed little interested in Thor, which he thought odd, considering how he charged in at them. Maybe they thought him too much of a barbarian to bother with. Their mistake. Thor killed one with a blow to the head with Mjolnir.

They must not have done their research.

The Chinese swept forward. Loki didn't think Odin really needed his help any more than Thor had. But --

Two of the Chinese grabbed one of the Ravens. With a shout of triumph, they pulled him away while he struggled against the captors. One of them had pulled a sword and clearly intended to behead him on the spot.

No.

Loki shouted and rushed forward, shoving aside a row of startled soldiers and came almost to the midst of the Gods before he felt a sharp pain in his back. One of the blades had found him. He was lucky he hadn't lost his head already.

He reached the captured Raven and sent enough pure, primal force against the Chinese to plaster a few of them against the side of the ship. Thor and Odin reached him by the time he had started pulling the wounded Raven back. He looked around, worried because Torin wasn't there -- but then saw Torin and the other Raven held the exit. Good. He wanted out of here. He wasn't certain what the hell they'd tell the people who ran the station when they saw the damage.

He feared the wound had gotten a lung. He gasped for air, too weak already to do anything to fix the damage. Damn. Damn. However, he had gotten the Raven back. Probably stupid, since the Raven worked for Odin, but the loss would have left their leader half-blind, so to speak. Besides, the Raven didn't deserve to get killed in this stupid power play.

Damn. He wasn't going any farther. Each breath had become agony and he found himself no longer trying to draw the air into his wounded lung --

"Why the hell did he do that?" Thor demanded, grabbing Loki's arm when he almost went to his knees. "He's no friend of the Ravens!"

Odin stopped in front of Loki and looked him in the face, the stare of his single blue eye as unfathomable as always. This was not the last thing he wanted to see. *Sigyn* -- Gods, he regretted. . . .

"He did it," Odin said, his voice sounding hollow and far away, "because it was the right thing to do."

Odin reached out and touched his face. He almost jerked away out of reflex before the magic caught hold of him. *Healed.* Not completely, but he knew he wouldn't die now. He gave a nod of thanks, though he fought to remain conscious.

Time to go. Whatever the Chinese had wanted, they were not going to win this round.

CHAPTER FIVE

C hu Jong remained still in the suddenly quiet room. The only sounds came from the hint of servants moving, nameless and faceless who were honored to serve the Gods forever. Silk clothing rustled and the faint scent of orchids drifted through the air along with the smell of the *Ti Kuan Yin* tea. Five others sat at the long table, but Chu Jong had taken the place of honor without asking their leave.

None looked at Di Jun's empty chair.

They had watched a simulation of the battle laid out on the table before them; a puppet play, the Imperial Guards on the magical strings Chu Jong had in his hands. Tialong fought well for a creature so long in retirement. The soldiers, like the servants, were faceless things, and he threw them at the enemy without much concern for what they did. Others hand joined in, hoping for glory, and they had lost a minor God or two, little concern for any of them.

Chu Jong sat with his cup of tea before him, carefully studying the trail of steam that lent ethereal patterns to the air before him. He had stopped watching the battle played out in miniature on the table. What happened there no longer mattered to him.

The conflict had not gone as well as he'd hoped, though he had learned more than a few things from the confrontation. He could now more carefully weigh powers, determination, anger --

his and the other side's -- in what would happen next.

The others at the table finally began to move. He sensed their anger and trepidation. He glanced at the battle and saw how the Norse had gathered their wounded and retreated. A shame. He had thought they would abandon Loki at the very least, if not the Raven the Chinese had come so close to clearing from this play.

"This is not good," Li Jing said, his voice steady.

"*This* is not trouble," Chu Jong replied, pulling himself away from his private reverie. He had to take this group in hand and lead them along the path like children. "We know many things now, and none too soon."

"You talk as though time were slipping away. We have time for anything," Li Jing replied with a snort of derision, his hand resting on the pagoda beside him as though he petted some dog.

"Do we really?"

The others shifted, uncomfortable but silent. Chu Jong leaned forward and wiped away the scene of battle with a wave of his hand and with his other hand he conjured another vision, this time a star scape filled with colors and movement no area of space should ever experience.

"We are going to this place," he said with a nod towards the new scene. "And you know why, do you not? We are going because the shell cracks. P'an Ku awakes. He will rise soon and cast his wakeful eye on all humanity has done while he slept. We must be the ones who have control when this happens. We must be the ones who stand in perfection while he destroys all else."

"You think such paltry things will matter?" Red Coat asked with a wave of his hand at the simulation. "You think you can *fool* P'an Ku?"

"I think we can convince him we are his in spirit and we will serve him in this new age."

"Why do we need these others? These barbarians?" Li Jing demanded, emotion showing there at last. Finally a question with some thought, meaning at least someone here was awakening to the reality around them.

Which made Li Jing dangerous as well, but perhaps he could set the old coward against Red Coat and Monkey King and keep them busy. As a diversion, Li Jing might work very well. For now, though he had to answer questions.

"We have the Norse as a show of choice, my companions." Chu Jong did not say friends, not to this group. He would have as soon done away with all of them, since most of the time they were no better than the clods of dirt, the peasants in the fields. "When given a choice between such barbarians or us, P'an Ku will choose our august pantheon. We are stability, power and order."

The others shifted with a whisper of silk; uneasy, this group, despite such an elegant answer. Chu Jong stood. He had no more time to waste here. The Norse would follow where they went. He had wanted to lessen their number, but he had no doubt the Chinese would win over the barbarians when the time came.

"There will be an accounting for the evil you have done."

Chu Jong looked down the table at Monkey King and found a smile coming to his lips despite how much he hated this creature. "Not if we win," he replied. "The win will be shown I had chosen the Heavenly Path and set the universe to right. I saw the way ahead and I knew we must move. Di Jun placed himself in the way of such movement. He would have, as he had always done, awaited signs and outcome. *I am the sign.*"

Monkey King moved from seat to the arm of his chair, more animal than human. His too-long, hairy arms hung from his silken robe of gold and green and his bearded face showed more hair than was proper a God. He had changed during the long ages, more so than any of them. Monkey King had left the jungles behind and had started to *ape* the rest of them long ago.

He glared at Chu Jong without the serenity of the true Gods. This creature had never belonged with them, and did no more than provide entertainment now and then. He had stolen his immorality and Godhood and, when this was over, Chu Jong thought there might finally come a time of accounting for his impudent theft.

"Ancient, revered -- and blind." It spoke with a fully human voice coming from a face not quite what it should be. Red Coat, not surprisingly, nodded agreement. The two were troublemakers. "No one can control the heavens. Shall we tell tales of those of us who have tried? You have started us on a path without consulting anyone. What is your right?"

"Should I have consulted with the likes of you?" he demanded, tired of the creature already. "Should I have argued with you like a commoner haggling over dinner?"

Monkey King laughed, the sound of a wild thing in the jungle. "Argue with me? Oh no, our great, glorious and wise Chu Jong," he mocked and moved to sit on the table itself, impious and ignorant of anything fine. "Do you think you can control me? Or the Norse God who walks the same path as I do?"

He hadn't expected this one to figure out his plan so quickly, but he did no more than blink. "You think you can stop me? You'll try?"

"Yes."

"Why?"

"Because it is my nature to stand in the path of fools."

Their eyes met. Chu Jong considered the possibility he had killed the wrong God after all. Or perhaps there would be more bloodshed before too long. Not here, not this moment. The others would take such an obvious move against Monkey King as a sign of weakness, showing he couldn't handle a few unpleasant words.

"Perhaps you should consult with your Norse barbarian," Monkey King snarled with such utter disdain he shocked the others. "I think we are done here."

Monkey King walked away first and the others followed.

CHAPTER SIX

K oil (because he really wanted to be *Koil* right now and not return to painful older paths) wasn't fully aware of what happened around him. He fought his way to consciousness, focusing on Torin's voice as the young man grew more impatient, but not angry. He took the sound as a good sign; Torin had his father's temper sometimes, so matters couldn't be too bad if he remained relatively calm.

"Sure, go ahead and blast through the plates if you don't give a damn what happens to the rest of the humans here. If you destroy one plate, there's going to be panic and the station is going to have a serious vulnerability in the bays where they most need protection. You do this and I wouldn't expect much cooperation from Koil afterwards," Torin said.

Koil, who was being held to his feet, lifted his head and found the problem. A wall of metal covered the right and, when he turned his head, he found another not far away to the left. Of course Station Admin had dropped the bulkheads into place and sealed off the bay area when they thought they had a major breach in the hull. He couldn't blame them.

Left his group in a bad position, though. Especially him, trapped here with only Torin for protection. He thought about trying to heal more of his wounds, because he didn't want to be in this position, dependent on Odin --

Or not dependent on Odin after all. One of the Ravens

held him up. Koil felt oddly safe in the hands of these creatures who had always remained with Odin.

Thor had moved apart from the others, glaring at the massive metal plate, his hammer in hand. He could probably pound his way through, which might be the best use they had for him at this point. The anger had not lessened in Thor. Koil could feel the emotion like an ill wind pulsing with each he artbeat.

"Where -- Chinese?" Koil asked, his voice unsteady and his breathing painful. He didn't try to pull away from the Raven because he didn't want to fall flat on his face and have to wait for someone to help him again.

"Gathering behind us." Torin glanced towards the bay with a bit of worry. "This is not a good place to be."

Koil looked around the area, noting the walls and the numbers. He wanted to return to *Chaos* where there would be better protection. He wasn't certain the best way to get there, though. He could probably open an access door despite the seals in place. Maybe. Right now he couldn't be certain of his plebian abilities, let alone anything with magic.

"The Chinese are pulling back," Odin said with a glance towards the bay. "Not good."

"Not good?" Thor asked, finally looking away from the metal wall.

"No," Koil began and took a deeper breath. "Because we are between the plate and void when they pull away. And you can bet they are not --"

"Not going to wait for a clearance from admin," Torin finished for him with a nod. "Damn."

"I can get us to *Asgard*." Odin lifted a hand towards the bay where the other unusual craft sat. "It won't be easy."

"Up to *Chaos*," Koil argued. There was no way he would go on board *Asgard*.

"I can't," Odin replied and Koil looked at him with shock

at the admission, never mind what it meant. Odin admitting to a weakness? The universe should have stopped right then. "You have too many shields and protections in place. I would take too long to pull them down. I could punch straight through them, of course, but that would create a problem."

"Like taking half the station out with us," Koil mumbled. Damn. Figured he'd be foiled by his own protections. He couldn't drop the wards from here, not in the state he was in. No choice. "Let's go. *Asgard*."

Odin touched the metal wall beside him, his fingers tracing the pattern of a dozen runes on the surface. Koil hadn't been around such strong magic in a long time; his breath caught as the power moved reality aside without destroying it. A tunnel of rainbow light formed and, though he couldn't say he wanted to travel the magical path, he didn't argue when they started in. He could feel the power of the Chinese ship growing. They would quickly pull away, despite the danger to others.

Going to be a dammed mess all the way around.

The power in the tunnel tingled. Unpleasant, but not bad. Odin couldn't take them into *Asgard* itself for the same reason he couldn't make a tunnel into *Chaos*. Too many wards and magics hung around the huge, ancient ship. It reeked of home and mythic tales. They would get close to her in the bay and not damage the station doing it.

Torin moved to his side and helped keep him to his feet as they neared the ancient ship. Koil focused on him --

"Don't say it," Torin said before he could speak. "I'm not abandoning you."

He knew the young man's stubbornness, as well as his curiosity. Of course Torin wanted to go into the ship and see the ancient powers to which he had been born, but never touched. Koil didn't want him here, but he didn't pretend he could order Torin away.

They reached the bay and the airlock opened at a wave of

Odin's hand.   They walked in through a common-enough airlock, no different from what they'd find on any visiting ship . . . and then they stepped out into a hall which was anything but normal.

The insubstantial walls began to change as soon as they entered.   Koil had an impression of silver as frost rose in a filigree tracing over surfaces which seemed no more solid than clouds.   A wind blew past, cold as any northern winter had ever been.   Sounds rose and died, and shapes formed in the growing mist, only to fade away again.

"This isn't right," Thor whispered.   "This isn't right. *Asgard* is unsettled.   Throw Loki out.   We don't need this trouble!"

"It isn't me," Koil replied, holding tight to consciousness since he had come into the lair of the enemy.   He could feel the wound in his back and other pains, but he was used to controlling his emotions.

Odin gave him a startled glance and lifted a hand before he nodded.   "Not Loki.   We all need calm."

"We need him out of here.   We've survived without him." Thor glared, preparing for a real fight, and Loki was in no way ready for the confrontation.   Was Thor defending his domain? Afraid of an interloper?

Afraid of myths, truths and lies?

Loki saw a rush of angry faces hurrying their way; familiar faces he had not seen since Ragnarok.   The temperature dropped once more and this time the influence came from him. *Asgard* had always seemed a cold, forbidding place, now made worse by too many people shouting with more than a little anger aimed his way.   Old feuds surged to life in a heartbeat.   Torin looked surprised but remained steady at his side.   The boy knew the basics of what to expect --

Or maybe not, because in the next moment something happened, surprising even Koil.

The Valkyrie arrived, dressed in silver suits that might have been woven of ice and snow, their hair cut short like helmets around their lean faces, and their stares forbidding. A full dozen moved down the hall, everyone -- including Thor -- scrambling to get out of the way. The walls steadied around the women and the look on their faces -- such disdain -- stopped Thor from speaking.

"We will take Loki into our care," Skuld announced, facing Odin. "He is not safe with you and yours."

Loki wasn't certain he needed his paranoia nudged a little further into reality, but Skuld's words didn't surprise him or Odin. The Valkyrie surrounded Loki in a wall of silver and spears, cutting him off from Torin. He reached for the boy, though --

"He will be safe. Odin will give his word on it." Skuld faced Odin with a stare that brooked no argument.

Odin had never liked to be ordered, but he must have felt much the same as Loki did right then. This was not a time to mess with the Valkyrie. Odin gave tight-lipped nod of agreement. Oddly enough, Loki did feel safer in their company. He and the ladies had never had any real arguments.

"Torin --"

"I'll be safe," he said. He bowed his head. "I'll be careful."

The Valkyrie took Loki from the Raven; surprisingly gentle women, though warriors all and people he never wanted go up against. Odin looked troubled, which pleased Loki more. He had been tossed around, manipulated and dragooned into their war, so he was glad enough to annoy the entire group.

They walked down the hall, which became a different hall though they hadn't changed direction. The walls shifted to hues of gold as though with the light of a new day. He wondered how many others had ever been invited into the forbidden realm of the Valkyrie.

He was in no shape to question or argue, gasping with each step. He'd needed to get away from Odin and Thor so he could think clearly. He wanted Torin here as well, and Sigyn . . . though maybe not her, too. She might survive. He didn't think anything good would come from being on this damned ship.

They entered a warm room filled with colors and the scent of pine trees. Skuld settled him on soft pillows, her hands brushing along wounds, easing pains and healing some of the worst problems.

"It is not in our nature to be healers," Skuld explained settling near him. She had a steady voice and he felt calmer as he listened to her. "We can ease pains, but not fully heal. Be wise, Loki. Do not push the others so hard because we might lose you to the darkness when you are most needed."

He pushed himself up, blinking and trying to understand what she was telling him. The room made him dizzy, soft and warm and not fully realized; a place they had pulled out of the magic of *Asgard* and made for him. He appreciated their help. He had the feeling he wouldn't have survived long with Odin or, rather, with Thor. At least here he didn't have to watch his back.

"Thank you, ladies." He gave them the best, courtly bow of his head he could manage.

That won a laugh from all of them. He hadn't expected the reaction and the sound unsettled him, wondering what game they played. He'd never thought of the Valkyrie as the wild, dangerous women as others imagined them, but he never thought he understood them, either.

The image of wildness had been created mostly from the mortal's view: dire creatures associated with glory and death. Odd, he thought, when he considered how the Norse myths had been stuck in a rut of macho poisoning from the start. He wondered how these women became their judges.

Skuld leaned closer, drawing his wandering attention. "We want your help."

Loki blinked, forcing himself to focus. This could be

dangerous. He moved and she pushed pillows in around him. He could see worry in her face. Was some of the worry for him or for other problems? Perhaps both.

"What can I do to help?" he asked. He had *not* offered the same thing to Odin. He hadn't thought to offer his help there. But here -- ah, *but here* they did not come demanding anything of him -- and *they* had never betrayed him.

Another Valkyrie crossed the room and settled on a pillow before him, her eyes downcast for a moment, which was far too demure for this woman who had led the Valkyrie since before history. Freyja was no cosseted princess and he didn't know what to make of this behavior. He did realize she'd stayed aside until he offered to help.

"We do not . . . we do not often ask for help," she admitted softly. Loki wondered if they had *ever* asked for help and didn't want to know the answer. He gave a slight nod, encouraging her to go on. He didn't trust his voice and he was too often apt to say witty and inappropriate things. Best to let Freyja tell this tale.

"We want Frigg back, Loki. We *desperately* want Frigg back. Her good sense and wisdom has held *Asgard* together, you know. Her ability to see trouble spots in the future allowed Odin to circumvent a number of problems. Without her and the Ravens --"

"Which is why they went for one of the Ravens, too." Loki had suspected the reason, but hadn't put the attack together with the loss of Frigg. They were, truly, trying to blind Odin. "I have already decided to do what I can to help get her back."

"Have you really?" Her deep blue eyes stared into his; he saw age and wisdom along with a smoldering fire longing for battles to return again. He knew the fire too well and had tried to bury the flames deep in himself. She tilted her head and read his soul. "Have you truly committed yourself?"

He looked away this time. "I don't want to be part of

another fiasco like the last one. I don't want to come away from this one as bitter as I was by the end of the last saga."

"And would you turn you back on the chance to help a friend?"

"No." He took a deeper breath. "No, I wouldn't."

"Frigg had seen things coming. She told us there was worse than the Chinese out there."

The prophecy threw him. He hadn't expected more trouble, or at least not different trouble. "What else?"

"She didn't say. I don't think she quite knew yet," Freyja admitted, giving a slight wave of her hand. One of the others brought them tea and cakes. The newcomer showed more consternation than Freyja and Skuld, which meant the others were not truly accepting of his appearance in their realm. He gave a bow of his head and remained polite. "Frigg only said things would change and change again. She said we should trust you."

"Oh, did she?" He gave an unexpected laugh, but gasped at the pain from the wound, not nearly healed enough. "No one does, you know. You don't trust me, despite Frigg's words."

A nod of agreement. Freyja wouldn't lie to him because she had no reason to. He knew anything the Valkyrie told him would be the truth, as far as they knew it. What they'd told him so far was not very good. More trouble? Something beyond the rebirth of a Chinese God who might, with a wave of his hand, destroy everything?

What the hell did all these people -- Norse and Chinese -- want with *him*? There was the question he hadn't truly thought through yet. He'd been too busy being paranoid. Now he had to back away and think about what he could bring to the table. The moment he pursued those lines, the answer became obvious.

He brought chaos, of course, though he didn't think anyone wanted his power fully released. Maybe they took hold of him to keep such a thing from happening. If they had wanted chaos, they would have stepped aside and let P'an Ku take back his creation. Well, as much *his* as this reality belonged to any of the elder creation Gods. In another age, someone else might have this role. So . . . so the Chinese might not be happy about their own creation God awakening because they knew he was not going to be happy with what he saw.

Loki wondered if the Norse expected him to fight chaos with chaos. If so, they were all fools. That way lay total destruction.

Or perhaps his role was different. The Chinese were all about structure and rules, like the soldiers they'd sent out; all perfectly in line, all ready to leap forward as one and never move out of the ranks. Loki had sent chaos against them and broken the symmetry, giving the Norse an edge. He couldn't believe he would have as good of luck with the Chinese Gods themselves, though.

And why did they want Frigg?

He leaned back, eyes narrowing as he worked his way through the labyrinth of events.

He felt the ship shudder as power surged through the craft. Realization brought him to his feet in anger, pain momentarily forgotten. "He's pulling out of the station! Damn him!"

"Easy, careful with such words in this place!" Freyja warned, taking his arm when he started to sway.

"He has no right to drag me along. He has no claim on me."

Loki pulled free of her hold and headed out of the room. He didn't know the layout of this ship, but he knew where he wanted to go and *Asgard* shaped the way for him, which he found troubling in some ways. This was not *his* ship. However he rushed forward anyway, ignoring pains as his rage grew. Colors and cold swirled around him and he thought he could hear the roar of a wind as he passed, though he never felt it.

Odin met him at the door to the control deck with both Ravens at his back and Thor standing nearby, ready for trouble. Loki found Torin standing near the controls, giving him a tight-lipped nod.

"I didn't agree to go with you," Loki gasped the words, his voice filled with anger and pain. He feared he would go to his knees. Unexpectedly, one of the Ravens caught hold of his arm and helped steady him. He saw Odin give a little twitch of surprise. "Take me home or I swear --"

"The Chinese pulled out," Odin explained, his voice unexpectedly worried. "We dared not let them go, Loki. I had hoped they wouldn't run so quickly once they realized we were in *Asgard*, but we can't let them out of our sight."

"Maybe following them is what they want," Torin replied and Loki gave a quick, tightlipped nod.

"This could well be true. Should we let them go?" Odin asked looking straight at Loki this time.

He glared, knowing Odin was right.

Torin drew his attention. "The station management is up in arms. First about the damage the bay area and now two ships pulling out without authorization. They don't know you and I are on board, but it's going to be pretty obvious we're gone soon. We need to get word to Sigyn about what's going on. She's going to have to take the heat from Station Admin."

"She can handle the trouble," Loki said, holding back a hiss as a spasm of pain passed through his back. "She's handled worse. Get me a line to Admin."

He spoke those words directly to Dion, knowing he was pushing the line. No one ordered Dion. *Odin.* Damn, even he was getting confused and he wanted to go with the names of the new age. Dealing with Dion was far less dire than dealing with Odin. They all had too much invested in the past.

"Get him a handheld link, Thor," Odin said.

Thor stared in shock, expecting a different reaction after

Loki's order. It was worth the moment. One of the Ravens handed him the device. Did he see a bit of a smirk at the corner of the Raven's mouth? My. Maybe a few too many centuries with Thor had taken a toll on relationships.

Loki punched through a call to Admin and was put straight through to the Station Master's office. She was, predictably, outraged. Loki let the woman rant until she ran out of breath.

"The entire incident is unfortunate." Loki kept his voice calm and serene. "However, we were only moments from something far worse."

"Worse?" Station Master Kikko asked, a slight catch in her voice. They'd had a few disagreements through the years, but the overbearing woman knew she could trust Loki.

"The other ship would have returned and attacked. If we had remained attached to the bay, the Station would have taken considerable damage." Another little catch of breath. At least he had her attention. "My . . . companions, with whom I now find myself traveling, had come to warn me of trouble," Loki continued. He dared not look at the others because anger would have become too plain in his voice. "We had not expected such outrageous behavior, however. This was far over the line. We will try to settle this matter elsewhere where other lives are not at stake. In the meantime, *Chaos* will cover half the cost of repairs to the station."

"Oh." He had shocked Kikko with the decision. The credits would help maintain a good relationship in the future. Loki had wealth enough to buy some peace of mind.

"You know I'm good for my word. I hope we can have this settled amicably and all will be well."

"Thank you." Kikko sounded far calmer than when this discussion started.

Loki keyed the connection off and frowned. "I need to let Sigyn know what to expect."

Odin nodded. Thor looked more irate. Good. He keyed

in a direct connection to her --

"Tell me you are *NOT* on the ship with those bastards!" she shouted as she came on line. "Tell me you and Torin aren't both --"

"No choice, Sigyn. Calm." He kept his own emotions in hand, wishing her peace and the ability to see this problem through.

"I will not be calm. You know you can't trust them!"

"And should I trust the Chinese more?"

A pause. "No. And they wanted their hands on you as well. Damn them all."

"This was inevitable and we both know it. I'll handle this matter as best I can and return as soon as possible. However, you are going to be dealing with Kikko."

"Hell. She has to be tearing her hair out."

"She was until I told her that *Chaos* would pay half the repairs."

"Ah."

"You are going to have to deal with it. Make her happy. I want to be able to come home."

He heard a slight sigh. Neither of them said what they both thought -- that they might not see each other again in this life. They would meet at some other time, though. He would always come home to her. It had nothing to do with old legends and circles.

"Take care," she whispered, her voice softening. "Both of you take care."

"We will."

He keyed the link off. Regretted doing so in one way, but he didn't want to say anything too personal with the others standing so close by. They were no longer a part of his life and he didn't want them sharing any of the joy he'd found.

He should have said goodbye at least. He handed the link to the Raven with a nod of thanks.

"We will bring you back," Odin promised, which he had not expected. Odin's word was good. "Providing, of course, any of us survive. I don't know where they're going --"

"Tracking on Draco systems," one of the Ravens said. They had rarely spoken before and hearing the low, soft voice gave Loki a bit of a chill.

"Draco. *Dragon.* That will be another link to their power," Odin replied. He shook his head. "We're late lining up our own myths."

Torin moved to stand by Loki. "There's been a disturbance in the Draco sector." He appeared to have gotten his anger in check, though the wall nearest him fluttered red and black. "I saw the information on the station feed this morning, Koil. They fear a sun is going to go supernova and probably take a couple more with it, along with several settlements."

Loki nodded and tried not to slouch. He hurt like hell and the anger hadn't helped. He had known Odin wouldn't return to the station, but he couldn't go without a protest. They had to follow the damned Chinese who had Frigg because *Asgard* might not catch them in time if they held back now. Loki, though, would much rather not have been part of this new power play in a game he didn't fully understand.

Thor growled words beneath his breath before he turned to Odin, his face red with rage. "He doesn't deserve to be treated well. He isn't on our side. He never was. If you left this to me, I'd dump him in space the first chance I got."

"You better listen to me." Loki's voice became dangerously quiet and a breeze grew, threatening to become a blizzard. He took a step closer to Thor, whose hand went to his belt knife. Mjolnir was nowhere in sight. "If I don't return to the station, you're going to feel a curse I've been building for centuries. And if you pull a weapon, you'll be feeling the curse from the Other Side. And believe me, you will still feel it. I've shaped this one especially for you, Thor."

"Don't you dare threaten me --"

"Get your boy in hand, Odin, because I'm already not in a good mood."

"Thor --" Odin started.

"We had to *drag* him onto the ship. He didn't want to come. And you trust him?"

Odin smiled, which annoyed both Thor and Loki this time. "He would have come anyway, Thor. He would never have walked away from the battle. It is his nature."

Odin put a hand on his son's shoulder and pulled Thor back. Torin looked at Loki, eyebrow raised. He gave a little signal they used at *Chaos* which meant to keep an eye on someone. The Ravens noticed. They remained silent when Torin followed Odin and Thor as the two left the room. Odin noted him and gave a slight nod of welcome. The Ravens followed behind the group.

This was a dangerous place for Loki. He shouldn't be on this ship, and all the more so since he wasn't certain a Chinese had been the one who attacked him from behind. Odin? Thor?

A Valkyrie moved to stand beside him. *Guard*. He went with her through *Asgard* while the walls changed around him, reshaping and coloring to suit his mood: dark and dangerous.

CHAPTER SEVEN

Well, hell.

Never in Torin's life had he expected to find himself standing on the fabled *Asgard* with his grandfather and father (neither of whom probably realized their relationship) as the magical ship pulled away from the station. Hell, hell, *hell*. He didn't trust the two, of course; he'd learned the mistrust from Koil. But he knew, like his adoptive father, they'd had no choice but to go along with this mess. The Chinese were, unexpectedly, a worse enemy than the rest of the Norse.

Torin didn't know where he should go since the Valkyrie didn't take him with Koil. He was rather glad of that, to be honest. They'd looked fierce and were not a group he wanted to annoy. So he kept back from the controls and focused on the screen, watching drones carting supplies along the station's lines, seeing normalcy already returning as they moved away. He could sense a lot of wild magic in the area, but the power would dissipate and, with the Chinese and the Norse pulling out, the station should be fine. The only magic left behind was carefully contained in *Chaos*.

He dared a glance at Odin and Thor. From the way Odin looked at him, he suspected his grandfather knew the truth about his lineage after all. Maybe he was mistaken, but there was appraisal in the stare and not the kind of look he would have given to someone of no importance to him. From Thor's look -- not really so certain there. Thor wouldn't be any happier with Loki's son than he would be with his own son raised by Loki. At least Torin knew better than to trust them, which left him in a strange and dangerous place right now.

"Station Admin wants to speak to Koil," someone said.

He decided to stop being a wallflower, which was not in his nature anyway. "Tell them Koil is not available but Torin is here." He stepped towards communications.

Thor made a move. Odin stopped him and gave a nod.

In a moment, he heard a familiar voice. Shelby sounded more than exasperated, and he could hardly blame her. He felt much the same way.

"What the hell is going on?" she demanded. "We have damage to a full bay, ships leaving without clearance, and very, very odd things going on with our vid systems. What do you know about it, Torin?"

"Not much I can tell you, Shel," he replied and truly wished he could. "The crew of the other ship came after Koil. Our friends arrived to warn us about the possibility of trouble." Best to keep to the story they'd begun.

"Why did they come for Koil?" she asked, though she sounded as though she might not really want to know. Wise woman, really.

"It's a very old bit of trouble Koil never expected to follow him here," he explained, the absolute truth, but still hiding deeper truths. "Nothing illegal. The other ship was way over the top in this."

He glanced at Odin and Thor, who both watched as though they were trying to parse some code he used. He decided this had better not go too long or there was no telling what might happen. "Why did you want to talk to Koil?"

"The truth? The station master was trying to figure out if you two were there of your own free will and, if not, what we should do about it."

The entire room went still. Odin blinked and the Ravens straightened. Thor's mouth fell open. It was such a comical sight that he had to turn away and take a quick, deep breath.

"No, nothing like that, Shel. We needed to get the trouble away from the station. You saw what happened. There were too many people in danger for us to go running around playing cowboys."

"There's more going on." Her voice held an obvious note of concern and he thought he heard the station master in the background. He wondered what they thought they could do against a ship already heading away.

"Come on, Shel," he said with a laugh, determined to keep them calm and hoping to allay some of their worries. "This is *Koil*. There's always more going on. But really, there's nothing more I can tell you. Don't worry. We plan to come home as soon as we can settle the trouble . . . elsewhere."

"I get the feeling I don't want to know what you plan to do."

"Does it help to know we don't actually have a plan?" he asked.

That won laughter from Odin and from Shelby.

"Okay," she answered, still sounding uncertain. "I'll talk to you when you get back."

"Lunch," he said, meaning it. He wanted some normality in his life.

"Sounds good."

The link went dead. He handed the device to the person at the comm station and looked around.

"They would have tried to come and take the two of you back," Odin said.

"Maybe." He shrugged.

"They are followers without belief."

"It's called *friendship*."

Thor snarled. Odin tapped him on the arm, but Torin didn't think Odin could hold Thor's temper in check much longer. Torin had never seen anyone so ready to explode before and knowing the power in that creature --

No, no. He backed away from the thought as quickly as he could. Thor was no different than Koil. *Than Loki*, which made him very much akin to other humans, only with a little something extra. Torin knew he harbored the same seed of magic in himself, though he rarely let the magic grow into true power.

The seed came from Thor, not from some *creature*. Thor was an angry man who had lived with lies for far too long. Torin wanted to feel sorry for him but, if he did, he thought such feelings would betray Koil.

"What now?" he finally asked.

"Tyr, find him quarters, if you would. Make certain the Valkyrie know where to find him so Loki doesn't get upset."

"Kick them both out the airlock," Thor mumbled.

"I don't think you really want to try that," Tyr replied with a laugh as he stood from one of the stations. Someone else slid into his place. They knew how to handle ships. "Shove Loki out an airlock? You think you'd survive? Torin, is it? Come on. I'll find you some rooms. Or make some."

Tyr grinned and headed out. Torin followed, without a bow of his head to the others, though he felt odd as he slipped past Odin. They were barely out in the hall before Thor began to yell.

"There's someone who's not happy with life," Tyr said and gave another laugh. "But that's no surprise. He never is."

"I suspected as much," Torin admitted. He knew more of why Thor was unhappy than Tyr, but this wasn't his tale to tell.

Tyr gave Torin an odd look. "You aren't human."

"Not entirely."

Tyr asked nothing more. "I'm going to move you to the

area closest to the Valkyrie. They're an odd bunch, but I would suppose living with Loki has you used to oddness." He moved one gloved hand -- not real, Torin realized. That would be the one Fenrir bit off. He tried not to feel a chill at such barbarity. He had to remember these were very old Gods and didn't have the same connections as the people he was used to dealing with on the station. He had spent his entire life with Sigyn and Koil, though. He wasn't entirely immune to oddness in his life; Tyr was right about that part.

"Here. This will do." Tyr touched the wall and things changed and melded, remade and reshaped. A door appeared and opened to a modern room, high tech, and nothing real. He didn't pause as he went inside, though. Tyr stopped at the edge of the door and looked around. "Good. I haven't lost my touch, so to speak. The comm unit will connect with the control deck. I'll be there for the duration of this trip. Let me know if you need anything. I'll be more than happy to help."

"Why? Because Odin put you over me?"

"Because . . ." Tyr stopped and looked distant as he stared at the silvery walls of the room he had created. The colors shifted slightly and returned to silver when Tyr shook his head as though to dispel his own thoughts. "Because we used to have a reputation for hospitality, you know. Sometimes I like to think we can still have some of the good things back. It wasn't all bad, the old times."

He walked away, the door sliding shut behind him and leaving Torin even less certain about his place in life, let alone on this magical ship.

CHAPTER EIGHT

Red Coat spotted Monkey King as he hurried along the path, heading to where Red Coat sat on a footbridge, dipping his toes in water and watching the koi dance beneath him. Red Coat thought he might enjoy being a koi for a while again. He'd tried that . . . oh, eons past. He'd found life in the water pleasant. Not at all the sort of thing others would expect of him, given his bloody past, but such ancient history had been eons ago as well. He'd grown and changed. Not many others on this craft bothered to look for choices. Monkey King did, but not always for the better.

He thought to leap and change as Monkey King sauntered closer. He knew from the look on the almost-human face that this meeting could not mean anything good.

"So, you sit here while the universe goes to hell?" Monkey King demanded and sat beside him, peering with a bit of amusement at the koi; *everything* amused Monkey King.

"P'an Ku awakes," Red Coat reminded him.

Monkey King nodded. "And now we know why Chu Jong has been so busy of late."

"Do we?" he asked. He couldn't parse it. "What would Chu Jong think to do --" Suddenly he knew the answer and understood Chu Jong's ambition. He started to stand. Sat down again. "He can't think to control P'an Ku, can he? I always thought him ambitious, but not mad."

"Only a very fine line divides one from one to the other," Monkey King replied, looking away from the koi. He sounded too serious. Red Coat was used to his companion's laughter. He welcomed the time spent with Monkey King, who had taught him how to let go of his past and how to be irreverent, which was a gift the others lacked. "And the rest do not truly awaken, preferring to dream of other imaginary times. Nothing was ever as good as they pretend. They follow without thought. Chu Jong wants to reshape the human realm into his control."

"Damn." Red Coat kicked at the water with his bare toes, startling koi into a panicked retreat. He glared at Monkey King, annoyed to find his quiet reverie had been interrupted by something which truly required his attention. He hadn't needed to work for a long time and gave a grimace of distaste. "I suppose you and I ought to do something then, yes?"

"I thought we might get drunk," Monkey King suggested and stood, not as tall as Red Coat and he tended to slouch, ape-like, at times. "Drunk for a good long time and watch the stars go down in glory."

"Or we could try to stop Chu Jong," Red Coat suggested.

"Maybe." Monkey King shrugged. "Let's go have a drink and think about it."

"Or maybe two," Red Coat agreed.

As they walked away, the bridge, the stream and the koi disappeared into the fog of nothingness. Red Coat sighed. He hoped he had a chance to call the scene back later and enjoy the calm.

He hoped they survived.

CHAPTER NINE

Time moved in eddies and danced on winds; the passage of hours and days swept forward and circled around her while she sat in the white, blank room and cast the runes across the table.

The ancient pieces of rock, carved by her fingers and worn thin by use, circled and spun in a vortex of now and tomorrow, of reality and chance. Nothing settled. She gathered them again and the old worn stones vibrated as they rested in her hand.

Frigg knew change was coming, of course. She had known so before she walked away from *Asgard*, though she hadn't seen anything clearly and had hoped going to the Chinese would give her a better link. Unfortunately, the Chinese remained a blank slate to her, except for a few. Chu Jong came clearest in her mind and she cast out the runes once more, thinking about him.

They settled this time, though showing nothing good. She read determination in those signs. She read folly, loss, *chaos* -- but she couldn't decide if those readings were for Chu Jong or what he left in his wake.

Frigg pulled the warm shawl over her shoulders, frowning at the runes which had so rarely failed her. She knew the fates of all people. That was easy; either you were mortal and destined to die . . . or you were not. The little steps were harder to see, especially in times of such flux. Everything changed too quickly now. She felt something stronger out there, beyond the drama they played out in this odd corner of the universe. Not P'an Ku, though he was trouble enough. Something she couldn't understand, so she let the thread go, concentrating on the current problem instead.

Two other Chinese came into her mind. An odd pair. She thought one a fancy pet, dressed up to be human . . . no, no. God enough. Monkey. Monkey King. He and the other . . . Red Coat. Luck. Interesting pair. They created a new ripple in the vortex. She tossed out the runes, with no better reading, though a different path at least. Some of the future might be less chaotic in their wake.

Odd, since she knew Loki now moved as well and brought more chaos with him. Her heart pounded harder at the thought. She could feel him at the edge of her thoughts, a touch of something oddly missed.

Frigg couldn't get a clear fix on him or what he intended, but she'd always had such trouble. She'd enjoyed his company when he wasn't in one of his moods. Sometimes he had astonished her with something unexpected. In a life where she could see the future path too clearly, he'd brought her the gift of surprise.

Loki should not have cut off her hair, but in doing so he had proven he could move outside her sight. The realization had frightened her at first, and later intrigued her.

And then everything went to hell.

Frigg gathered the runes and put them away in a worn leather bag. She let the room swirl with a hint of cold and ice; better the cold than the emptiness she felt there at the edge of her sight. She didn't sense the emptiness of space, but rather a future without anything. All gone.

She didn't intend to let things go that way. For now, there was not a lot she could do except sit and wait. *Patience.* She had learned the trait eons past but, with everything in such flux, she found herself anxious. Worried. Everything was going to change.

CHAPTER TEN

C hu Jong moved from elegantly painted walls with hand-woven silk hangings to the bare silver and black of the upper decks. A thin line of mist parted before him as the old world gave way to the new. The sounds and scents changed and, though he disliked this new place, he did not shirk from coming here.

The area reeked of power, though many of the others would never have realized. Power ran through the very metal of the walls, a dull throb mimicking the heartbeat of a mythical monster, soon to come to life. Tialong radiated a power to propel the ship through the stars, though today he felt an undercurrent of sullen unease.

Chu Jong put his hand to the wall. *Be calm. You will have another chance at the Norse.*

The dragon settled somewhat.

Chu Jong brushed his clothing, exchanging silken robes for the black and red uniform with the dragon insignia on the collar. At the next curve, he came into the control deck. People saluted and the Captain crossed the room to give him a very low and proper bow.

He surveyed the room, taking note of the few who worked their stations, chosen to serve eternity with the Gods of their ancestors. Blessed . . . so long as they remembered their place.

"Sir," Captain Bohai said, his voice soft. "The Norse ship

has pulled out and is following us."

"Excellent." Chu Jong smiled; he didn't do so often, especially here on the control deck. The smile startled the man, who almost took a step backwards. Chu Jong took the moment to look over the control panels, pleased to see everyone hard at their job, though he understood none of what they did here. He would rather have left the ship's functions fully to magic and in the power of the Gods, but they needed this show of human technology to put in at ports.

They needed the connection to those places where mankind had spread among the stars. They would have disappeared into the void without some contact with humanity. The Norse knew enough to maintain a link of their own. Even the egocentric half-blind Greeks and Romans had finally figured it out. They could exist in the void, but what would be the use? No power. Nothing more than mere existence, and in such a state they might as well be human and die instead.

The Captain would never understand why he should be so happy about the Norse. So blind.

Chu Jong gave a benevolent nod towards these almost-mortals, as though they would count in the matter. "We go to face P'an Ku, who is the One Before All. We go to show him how we are civilized and wise. P'an Ku has slept long and when he awakes, he will find things much changed. What we understand as the wider universe and the spread of humanity will look only like so much chaos to him. We do not want P'an Ku to make a sudden decision."

"But . . . the Norse?" the man asked, waving a hand towards the screens where they could watch the other ship with their *technology*. He needed no such tricks. He could feel the Norse and their magic, a glowing shadow behind them.

"How can the First God judge how civilized we are if there is nothing in comparison? Shall he not look upon the Norse and wipe them from the universe and then smile upon us?"

The man's eyes brightened.

"We shall be the ones in charge when P'an Ku creates the new order," Chu Jong announced, his voice steady and loud. "We are the ones who will spread order and civilization through the universe and raise the humans out of the chaos they have wallowed in, like recalcitrant children. We will have the power."

I will have the power. However, he felt magnanimous today and spread a little of his blessing to these people. Unlike the half-blind Gods below, they at least listened to him and believed. He should, perhaps, spend more time with them. *His people. His followers.* The others, in the end, would envy him --

Movement at the entrance behind him: he turned and managed not to curse. A man in the Emperor's livery entered carrying the Banner of the Emperor. Damn! And the pretentious human held a proclamation as well.

Everyone stood and bowed very low, including Chu Jong who knew one must always hold to form. They were civilized and respected the hierarchy created in the ancient days. Oh yes, even the Gods bowed . . . at least here, in this place where they were seen by the near mortals.

"In the name of the Eternal Emperor," the messenger said, his voice sonorous, filling the room with a whisper of ancient days and old powers. "The ways of the heavens are wide, but the path is true. The gates of eternity are before us and we shall lead the way to righteous victory. Destiny is ours."

If he hadn't already been bowed before the banner, the symbol of the Emperor, Chu Jong might have given way to a show of shock. He had not expected the Emperor to *approve.* And now all he had to do was make certain he pushed destiny in the way he wanted.

By the time the messenger walked away with the banner, he had his emotions in control. The others scrambled into their seats, running checks, making certain nothing had gone astray in those moments when they all had to abandon work to bow before an old power and the symbol of their civilization.

"I will bother you no more," Chu Jong said.

"We are honored with your presence," the captain replied, giving a bow almost as deep as he gave to the banner.

Oh, yes, wise man. He knew where power rested.

Chu Jong gave a slight inclination of his head and turned away. He almost regretted leaving the technology behind this time. They did not question him here. Still, as soon as he was safely out of sight, he brushed away the uniform, glad to be wearing the silks once more. A pause only, to take in the scent of ages, to breathe in the tranquility of a place well-ordered and in harmony with the universe. Alas, this would not last. He must go to see Baldr once more and keep the barbarian placated in case he needed more information about the Norse. Besides, he found it odd -- though not horribly surprising -- that the man did not ask about the Norse whom he had to know were close. Baldr had tried to put a wall between himself and them. Did Baldr really think he could disown his past?

Fool.

He would not have use for Baldr much longer. The barbarian served his purpose by willingly linking Chu Jong to the Norse; Frigg would not do the same, but at least he partially blinded the barbarians by taking her.

He turned a corner and found himself, quite unexpectedly, facing a huge white tiger. A moment's shock gave way to a quick bow of his head. Po Hu was a messenger as well. When the tiger growled and started down a hall only newly sprung to life, he knew he had no choice but to follow. This was not where he had wanted to go, but one did not ignore a summons from the Queen Mother, the Guardian of the West, a being of immense power. He tread carefully before her notice.

Po Hu led him along a treacherous path that proved to be no trouble for the surefooted tiger. They walked through mists and he could feel wind off the mountains sweep in around them, cold and frightening as the path became encrusted in ice. Blowing snow all but blinded him. This was her realm and his own powers were uncertain in this place. She might hold the whole universe here in this icy wasteland and he could be lost forever if he did not stay close to the tiger.

The wind blew harder before dying a way to a soft icy breeze. He stepped into a room with clouds swirling in the ceiling, snow soft beneath his feet, and the Queen Mother sitting in her Jade Throne. He'd been here before, though by a different and less treacherous route. He was no fool, though, to complain as he quickly bowed.

Besides only Po Hu would see him. If the tiger smirked as he sat beside the throne, did it matter? The queen caressed the tiger's fur, her head tilted slightly, her lips pursed. Power radiated from her presence and to look upon her face was an act of will he couldn't hold for long.

"I am reminded of a tale, Chu Jong." Her voice held a whisper of winter that never promised the coming of spring. "An old tale by Chan Kuo Ts'e. I think you know it:

"A tiger trapped a fox, but the fox said, 'You dare not to eat me! The Gods of Heaven deem me the most important of all animals and you risk their wrath. If you doubt me, follow as I travel and see if any animal dares stand his ground.' The tiger agreed and followed close behind the fox and every animal fled. Amazed, the tiger agreed the Gods of Heaven had chosen the fox and so the tiger went on his way."

The wind blew cold against his face. He didn't dare to breathe as the Queen Mother leaned forward, her silver hair cascading across her white gown. Her dark eyes seemed no more than rocks of obsidian in a face as pale as snow. "Do not think yourself so smart, my little fox. My tiger knows the tale. Always remember who is standing behind you."

She gave a flick of her fingers, dismissing him. Fog filled the room and the wind roared. He could no longer see her. Po Hu nudged his leg and he followed the tiger along the treacherous icy path -- a far less dangerous place than to stand before her.

CHAPTER ELEVEN

S omeone knocked on the door.

Torin looked up from the desk, startled by the sound. He would have thought anyone on this ship would have known to use a buzzer to draw attention. Or perhaps not on this odd craft. Sitting here in a room which mimicked his own at *Chaos*, he had forgotten there were parts of *Asgard* that hadn't connected with technology, despite travelling across the stars. He suspected someone from such an area had come to seek him out. Was this a good thing?

The person knocked again. A polite knock, winning his curiosity.

Torin carried the laser pistol in the holster under his arm. He shifted the weapon slightly and went to the door. He could have ordered the door open, but he wanted to be closer in case trouble came through. He didn't trust the pistol to work well here.

Didn't trust much of anything here, in fact.

He opened the door with a touch of the button on the wall. The two people on the other side looked startled and possibly as uncertain as he felt.

"Yes?" he asked.

"You came with Loki," the young man said, his voice low.

Brown hair fell forward and covered his face as the stranger bowed his head, though Torin had caught sight of bright eyes and a sharp goatee. Perhaps not young, he realized . . . and possibly not really a man. Torin glanced from him to the woman, dressed in a long black dress, her hair as dark as night and her eyes glittering as though they held distant stars. She seemed distracted, no doubt by the spirits darting forward and whispering in her ears.

"Fenrir. Hel." He gave a polite bow of his head. "Loki doesn't know you're on *Asgard*, does he?"

"No," Hel replied and slapped away a persistent spirit circling her head.

"Come in." Torin stepped aside and gave a bow of his head, his fingers twitching and wanting to reach for the pistol. He knew about Loki's children, the ones who had survived and the ones who had seemed to disappear after Ragnarok. These two were powerful and dangerous.

They stepped slowly into the room, clearly not comfortable. Fenrir sniffed, his eyes narrowed.

"This isn't like the rest of the ship." Fenrir gave the room a nervous glance.

"It's the world I'm used to," Torin replied. He waved them to the chairs. "Is there anything I can do to make you more comfortable here?"

"The room is nice," Hel said and surprised them both. "I grow weary of living in the same old world, don't you, Fenrir?"

"I grow weary of a number of things," he answered and brushed aside his hair, uncovering a sharp face and restless amber eyes. Torin wondered what Fenrir looked like in his wolf form and suspected he was probably much the same as in this lean, restless body. Hel seemed darker. Torin felt an odd tingle when he saw her resemblance to her father, Loki. Did he look like his own father?

"What can I do for you?" he asked as he sat at the desk. He couldn't imagine there was anything he could offer, but he was curious. Some called Loki's real children monsters, but that --

again -- was part of a legend tainted by lies long ago. These two were *different*, though.

"We know Loki came here against his will. We don't know where he is now, though. I sense he is on the ship, but where?" Hel asked. She glanced around. "I had hoped to find him here."

"The Valkyrie took him into their care."

The two stared. He'd been right to think something odd when the Valkyrie took Loki. He wondered if Loki was as safe as he had hoped.

"Hiding him from the others," Fenrir said and gave a bright grin. "Oh and Thor must be at wit's end by now, knowing Loki could be saying . . . things."

"I know the truth of what happened," Torin said.

"You are half Aesir." Hel leaned forward, her long fingers raised to touch the air. "Not blood of our blood. Not Risi. You are not either Loki or Sigyn's child, are you?"

"No." He stopped for a moment, but hiding the truth would be unwise. "I'm Thor's son. Thor doesn't know."

Fenrir's eyes went odd and Torin feared he would face the wolf in a moment. Damn. Hel tapped her brother on the arm and Fenrir shook his head and frowned, calmer again. She stared at Torin, her head tilted as she sent the spirits away with a wave of her hand, which made him rethink what they might be. Not pests; he suddenly suspected spies.

"You were with him. He raised you, didn't he? Why?" she asked, leaning forward, more clearly connected to *here* than she had been before. "Why would our father do such a thing?

A pretty woman, when you saw her clearly, this person who gave her name to hell itself. He smiled and she seemed less worried now. "He hunted for a child to have his revenge," Torin admitted and sat back. "He raised me to be everything Thor is not."

"And you are not bitter," Fenrir said. It wasn't a question.

"I've had a good life. Loki and I work well together. He

confessed his feelings changed over the years. He says I remind him more of my father when they were friends, which I take as a good sign and a compliment."

"I hadn't expected such a surprise," Fenrir admitted. He settled in the chair, his lanky body relaxing, and the feel of having a wolf in the room dissipated somewhat. "Maybe that's good. When did life start being so easy with nothing new and no challenges?"

"When we came to *Asgard*," Hel replied.

Fenrir nodded agreement.

"Why are you here?" Torin dared ask. He never would have expected to find any of Loki's children on *Asgard*, especially these two who knew the truth about the myths.

"I realized I couldn't fit in anywhere else," Fenrir explained. He blinked and stared at the wall. The room grew a little colder, a touch of the old winter returned. Torin was used to it, having felt the same from Loki sometimes. "I thought to go to Loki, but he'd taken residence in the station and seemed too far from anything wild and a place where I could fit. I didn't think I could live there. Here . . . here I can create the things I need sometimes. I can run in the woods. And they know what I am. I don't need to hide."

"And I could never hide," Hel added. She gave a shrug. The spirits were back, streamers of white taking human shape to whisper in her ear. She paused and listened, then sent them on their way again. "I don't mind. This is what I am. I think, though, something else is changing, even here on *Asgard*."

Fenrir gave her a narrow-eyed look. "Trouble coming, you mean. This whole business with the Chinese Gods and the games they are playing. So the Norse are called to do battle at the end of the world -- or the universe, this time. I hate the idea of having no choice. I hate fate playing such games with us again."

"Can we ever escape it?" she asked.

He snarled before his face changed and he sighed. "Maybe not."

"Is there anything you want me to tell Koil -- Loki -- when I next see him?"

Hel shifted in her chair, apparently anxious to be away again. "Tell Loki that Frigg knew about the Chinese and she went anyway. Tell him Frigg knew more of what is going on than any of us do, but she wouldn't say what was out there. I don't know why."

"I think she went because she didn't see wide enough here on *Asgard*." Fenrir glanced at Hel. Torin supposed a person could get used to the filmy, white creatures darting in around her. "What she knew might have been only enough to create greater problems if she didn't direct us on the right path. She was worried. I found her walking in my woods, you know. I told you so."

"Ah, yes. Looking for you, I thought."

"Yes," Fenrir replied, his amber eyes narrowed in thought. "But all she could say was to be ready for things to happen."

"Helpful as always," Hel mumbled. "But what should we expect? The old Gods are almost always more bothersome than helpful. And Loki is the worst of the lot of them, when it comes to creating trouble."

Torin laughed. Fenrir added a slight grin, though he looked bothered. Torin wondered if they would have felt better talking with a half-brother, or maybe someone who wasn't related to Thor. This wasn't the time to ask. He hoped he had time to know them better, though.

Fenrir's face grew serious once more. "Loki shouldn't be on this ship. He should never have been dragged into this problem."

"He couldn't hide, you know. They'd have found him. And . . . something tells me maybe this is better. He would never do well, standing back from the trouble. Besides, you can bet he's finally going to tell his side of the story about Baldr and all the rest of those lies."

"Yes." Hel's dark eyes narrowed as more of the spirits swept in around, distracting her for a moment. She focused on him with obvious effort. "And that's why he shouldn't be here. He's only going to provoke them to anger, stirring up those flames again. Thor is ready to explode."

"Do you think Loki can take him?"

"Maybe. But I don't want to be around for the battle," she admitted. "None of us do. That could be a battle that would end worlds."

She had a point.

However, part of Torin really wanted Loki to have his chance at vindication. "I'm lost here." He looked from Hel to Fenrir. "This is not the kind of world for which I was trained. I know about *Asgard* and all the rest. I know *what* I am. I know who all of you are. I don't know how to fit into this world, though. So I have my modern room in a ship more ancient than man's first journey to the moon. I fit in this room. I don't know what any of the rest of this means."

"It means you are in trouble," Fenrir replied and grinned again. "Don't worry. Those of us who stand with Loki will stand together. I can't say what Odin will choose, though. I have noticed how he's grown weary of Thor of late, especially since Thor his grown more sullen and combative."

"Odin will do whatever best serves the myth," Torin said.

"Oh, you understand far better than I thought," Hel answered. She smiled. "And you do know enough to be careful."

"Yes." Torin stood with his visitors, sorry to see them leaving so soon.

"We'll see you at the feast tonight, I'm sure," Fenrir said.

"Feast?"

"Oh yes. There is a feast most nights, but there is bound to be a special one tonight since we are going to battle soon. The feast tonight is going to be far too much like the ones in the old days in Valhalla." Fenrir met his look and grinned again, a show of teeth that might have been a little too sharp. "Be sure you wear a weapon."

"Ah. Of course."

"In fact. . . ." Hel stopped by the door and looked distant for a moment. "In fact, you should come with us so the others see you are not without allies."

"And we are allies?" he dared ask, looking from one to the other again.

"Oh yes," Fenrir replied. "We have a few others who will stand with Loki, as long as he doesn't do anything too stupid."

"Oh, but if he does, that might be fun," Hel replied with a truly bright grin. "Would you join us?"

"Yes, thank you. I'm grateful for the offer and the warning."

"We'll come by and pick you up," Fenrir said. He grinned and Torin thought maybe the wolf-son had acquired Loki's sense of humor and adventure. He wondered how many others saw his father in Fenrir.

Torin escorted the two to the door, using the button to open it. They were both intrigued by that bit of technology. After they'd gone, he went to his desk. At least he knew what he would be doing tonight. Feast. He thought this might be . . . interesting.

CHAPTER TWELVE

"Time to go," Freyja said, leaning over the pillows where he'd slept.

"Go?" Loki sat up, moving slowly, and his mouth closed against the escape of any curse. Pain lingered, but he'd felt worse in the past. Oh, best not to think about the past now, though his finger traced a scar by his eye. The one scar stayed with him, through death and rebirth, and never went away.

"We go to the feast," she explained and gave a wave of her hand. His clothing changed to something neater, well-tailored and not old-fashioned. He could have done the same himself, but she clearly didn't want to waste time. Her blue eyes showed a hint of anticipation.

"Thank you." He got slowly to his feet, testing movement, breathing and balance. "Why did you take me in?"

"Frigg trusts you. You are important and Thor doesn't see -- doesn't *want* to see -- the truth. Best if you are ready to face him when the time comes."

"We have things to settle, Thor and I," he said. She didn't argue. "And a feast might be the best time for me to tell a very old tale. I don't want to go into battle without the people at my back at least knowing the truth."

"And knowing this truth will change what happens?"

"It will change something."

She asked no more as they walked along the long silvery hall, Loki the troublemaker in the company of a dozen Valkyrie. He couldn't decide what they really wanted from him. Was he important? Well, he'd never doubted his own importance, but that didn't explain why they thought him so. How did his needs and their plans intersect? What could he do for them? Why didn't they try to dissuade him from what he planned tonight?

The corridor began to transform as the formless icy walls gave way to Valhalla. This was not a magical copy of the ancient site of power, but the place itself. Valhalla followed Odin around like a puppy, hoping for attention -- but then, so did the other Gods. Loki needed to see whom he stood against in this battle. Not the Chinese; he knew them as enemies. Here, though . . . here he wanted to know which of the Norse would be a problem when trouble started and someone pointed a finger at him.

They always blamed him when matters got out of hand, but tonight they might be right. This time he intended take the first step and rip through the old myths rather than waiting to be the scapegoat to old lies. Bitter thoughts; they'd lingered with him for eons now and this was the time to act and banish the rage he'd held so long. He wanted to move on.

After this new war.

They entered the great hall through the north door, of course. Loki had expected the room to be more archaic. However, the place had mutated into something of a more modern age, though he could see the hint of spears and shields in the ceiling as well as a suggestion of wood in the tables. Not smoky, though he caught the scent of burning pine and could hear the crackle of the fire. Mugs of ale sat at every table, along with choice cuts of meat and a scattering of vegetables. He thought Andhrimnir must have outdone himself tonight because Loki suspected the Gods were not served any better. The chosen feasted with delight and rigor. He thought, perhaps, they had been too long away from the battle, always waiting to be called back to service.

Coming through the north door settled his nerves and infused him with a whisper of old powers. This area was linked to the Old World more surely than anywhere else he'd been on the ship. Power clung to the space and drifted on the scents of things long gone.

He hadn't expected to find Fenrir and Hel waiting for him.

"Father," Fenrir greeted him, a soft growl of sound as he stepped closer. Loki always saw a bit of wolf in him, even in his full human form. "We suspected you'd be here tonight."

"Little choice," Loki admitted with a glance at his escorts. "But why are you two here on *Asgard?* You never had any ties with this group."

"The myths always call us back," Hel replied. She waved away a filmy spirit. They clustered around her and he suspected time and space meant nothing to them.

"Does anyone ever escape to something better?" he asked, curious because she might actually know.

"Very few. We who are connected to *Asgard* are almost always drawn back. This is what we are," she said with a glance around the room where others began to note his arrival.

Fenrir, surprisingly, shook his head in disagreement, shaggy hair falling across his amber eyes. "No, Hel. Not *what we are*, but rather too much of what we *want to be*. Without the myths, what are we? Nothing more than your companions, a whisper of life lost."

Loki hadn't expected such wisdom from Fenrir. "I want things to be different this time," Loki said. The words sounded odd, perhaps. They both frowned. "I think we might start with the truth, don't you think?"

Fenrir blinked and gave a wolfish grin. "Oh yes. The truth will make everything *different*. Do you really expect to survive the telling of this tale?"

He gave a shrug and wondered how much the Valkyrie would protect him. They had moved off, but not far, watching over the crowd like lovely, but demented, angels. "Odin and the others want me here for some reason so they won't be quick to kill me. Will you watch over the boy? Torin doesn't fully understand how treacherous this group can be. How dangerous. He never lived in the age of myth and no amount of tale-telling can truly prepare someone for this reality."

"We've already introduced ourselves. He's there at our table. He is not your son," Hel said. No surprise came to her voice. They both would have known blood of their blood.

"No he is not," he agreed and considered for a moment, but they needed to know the truth. "He's Thor's son."

"He told us," Fenrir replied. "We were surprised, both at who he was and his trust in us."

Loki hid his smile. "He is not Thor. He is someone whom I raised to be everything Thor isn't: trustworthy, dependable and honest."

"Everything Thor *should be*," Hel replied and met Loki's look more steadily than was usual from her. "Everything he had been before the end."

"Everything he had been," Loki agreed and won a nod from her. So he passed some test, though he couldn't be certain if this was one of truthfulness or not. He suspected it might be more about acceptance.

"I hadn't thought I'd have a chance to tell you." Hel leaned closer and her strange companions brushed across Loki's hair. He tried not to shiver. "Frigg knew there would be trouble with the Chinese, but she went out anyway. She wasn't happy, though. I think she saw something in the future that frightened her."

Not a good thing to hear --

"Loki!" Odin shouted from across the room.

"There is my queue to come on stage." He smiled and

probably looked no less ferocious than Fenrir. "Get ready for the show."

Loki sauntered across the room, weaving between tables. Odin, Thor and a few of the others sat at the far end of the room at a longer, more ornate table, placed slightly higher on a stage where others could clearly see them. Oh, yes, very much a show. Despite the change in the walls, this mimicked the old days, especially seeing the glint of anticipation in the eyes of some of the warriors as he passed their tables. The looks mimicked the expectation in the faces of those seated with Odin. More of them than he had expected, in fact -- Forseti, Kvasir, Nott, Eir and a dozen more he noted only as shapes because he dared not take his eyes from Thor and Odin for too long. The low rumble of an emotional tide swept in around him. He couldn't disappoint them now, could he?

"I wasn't certain you would join us." Odin gestured to a high-backed chair beside Tyr. Frigg's chair sat empty to Odin's left, a reminder that this wasn't all a game. The Ravens remained, statue-like, behind Odin's chair and watched him coolly, but Thor's face reddened and his hand curled so tightly around the golden goblet Loki expected him to dent the gold.

Loki sat at his appointed place and lifted a glass of mead, sipping and savoring the taste while he watched the others. Laughter rose along with shouts, everything echoing throughout the room; old songs began and ended amid roars of laughter. He fought against the feeling of having come home. He didn't want to find himself returned to those old fateful days, helpless against lies. He looked for changes and grabbed at anything to stop drowning in history. This place had better heating and acoustics and the Ravens wore all their tech toys. Things changed and the changes gave him strength.

He feasted, taking his rightful place among the other Gods; feasted on mead and venison -- now there was a trick, because this wasn't magic meat -- and for a while he relaxed and let himself be what he had been in another age.

He had no intentions of staying with the Norse, though certain aspects of being here appealed to him. They had been companions in better tales before the end. He saw Torin sitting with Fenrir and Hel and thought they made a good group -- a formidable group. No one would mess with them tonight, whatever Loki did.

There were myths about Loki that had always been true and he was about to confirm at least one of them. He did often create trouble and he intended to do so before this feast was finished. Odin expected the trouble and looked to Loki at every sip of mead as though wondering what was holding him back.

He didn't hear who called for a tale, but Loki had known the call would come. He was ready.

Loki stood. "I have a tale to tell." The room fell instantly silent, as though a single breath taken in and held. Forseti looked intrigued and perhaps the God of Justice had sensed something wrong for a long time. "This is a tale long overdue."

Thor started to stand, a curse at his lips. One of the Ravens pushed him back down.

Now *there* was a sign from the Gods. Loki smiled despite the story he meant to tell. Thor knew what he would say and his face had gone from red to white. The others noticed the change. The stillness grew in the room as though time itself waited to hear Loki's tale.

Odin said nothing at all.

"There was a place in days of old, far from the stars. A place some say was on Mother Earth, but in truth this was a different realm, a half-step away from the world of men, the two places tied forever together by myths and belief. There the old Gods ruled and lived in their archaic splendor. But the ages passed on, from good to bad and evil grew among them." He paused a moment and looked to Odin. "*Would you know yet more?*"

He heard the sound of surprise as he spoke those words from the *eddas*, the lines resonating in a time far beyond the first telling of those old tales. Would they know yet more? Oh yes. This was a tale almost all of them wanted to hear.

"This is the true tale of how Baldr died, *my friends.*" He didn't look at the others, but they listened, all of them. He stayed focused on Thor and Odin. Thor's face turned red once more, rage growing with each breath. Odin stayed very still, his emotions hidden behind a wall of ice. "There is a truth you should all know about the *best of the gods*, about our beloved Baldr. He had begun to believe too well in how much better he was than the rest of us. He went to the Roman Gods and offered to help them overcome us, because he thought them far more civilized than the rude, barbaric Norse. The Roman pantheon would have had no trouble subsuming the upstart North. They'd made an art of swallowing the myths of other Gods and spinning them out as their own."

A whisper of words spun through the room like a breeze newly born. He thought he would hear a hint of disbelief but all they had to do was look to Thor and Odin to know the truth.

"Shut up," Thor ordered, his voice a hiss of anger, the words hardly understandable.

"*Would you know not more?*" Loki taunted. Thor threw his goblet, but Loki batted the cup aside, the mead scattering in a golden spray and the goblet hitting the floor with the crash of an out-of-tune bell. The room fell silent as Loki continued. "Thor learned what his beloved brother had done and feared if the Romans listened to Baldr, those ancient and powerful Gods might easily overcome the newer powers of the north. He tried to talk to Baldr, but his brother would not rejoin the others. So Thor proceeded with another plan to remove Baldr before he could do any true harm. Ah, but to murder his own brother -- no, he could not do so and remain the great Thor. The act would, most likely, have caused more trouble than the Romans could create, at least in the short run. Besides, he didn't want the truth to be known about the beloved of the Norse Gods. He wanted to protect his family's legend."

Thor leaned back. Had he thought Loki never knew? Never figured out the reasons behind his betrayal? Loki glanced to the side and saw shocked faces mixed with understanding and dread. Oh, yes, they were beginning to understand a very old lie.

"It was easy to blame the perpetual outsider," he said with a brush of his hand across his own chest. His voice remained calmer than he had expected, given how long he had waited to tell this tale, dreaming of this chance. But now . . . now this became something more than justice. Now he thought the others needed to know for more reasons than his pride.

"We saw you and Hoor said you set him up to kill Baldr, taking advantage of the fact he was blind," Bragi snarled and leaned forward. Anger showed in his face. "What kind of game are you playing now, Loki? We talked to you. We knew --"

"When did all of you forget that I am not the only shapeshifter among the Norse Gods?"

Shock. Disbelief. But eyes turned -- oh yes, they turned -- to the person sitting beside Thor: Vali, the other son, who had been all but forgotten in the myths while Loki the outsider shone brightly. Vali was the shapeshifter son and someone Odin and Thor had never wanted others to consider for very long. They'd manipulated the tales until he was lost to almost all the legends, hiding his abilities. The later tales claimed he had been born to avenge the death of Baldr, but Vali had only been reborn to bury anything from the age before.

"Thor asked me go on a secret mission for him," Loki said with a tilt of his head. Thor looked at his hands, silent. Vali looked as though he might be ill but, oddly, he was the one who gave Loki the nod to continue. "I went; it was a trifling thing, but I had done such work for him before. By the time I came back, I learned I had been accused of Baldr's murder. Worse, they said I had not wept for him and condemned him to not return from death. Had I ever been such a fool before? Why would I turn everyone against me? Why would I put myself in a position to be hunted and tortured? *Would you know yet more?*"

Voices rose in protest for the first time, but Loki lifted a hand and silenced them. *Odin had denied nothing.* Thor was pale and Vali bowed his head.

"You have more to this tale?" Odin finally asked, his voice steady, his face without emotion.

"It's a tale you should have told long before now. You knew the truth. What is the use of having the Ravens if they couldn't keep track of your own murderous brood, right?"

And the Ravens nodded agreement, the act stilling even Loki. This was a sign and the kind that put a chill through him. He saw Odin give them a startled glance, not lost on the others. Odin gave a contemptuous wave of his hand. "It's an old tale, Loki. What does any of this matter now?"

He felt the heat rise this time and suspected Odin did so on purpose. Did he want Loki to lose his temper? Maybe so, but Loki had learned patience during his long life. He would not ruin the tale now.

"I see Thor. I see Vali," Loki said with a wave of his hand. "But where are *my* sons, Narfi and my Vali? You killed my sons and if they came back, I never saw them again. You tortured me. And you always knew the truth of what had happened. Now you come to me and expect me to fight for you and yours? I have a long memory, Odin."

"We have outlived those days," Odin answered, his finger tapping the edge of his goblet. "We're more civilized now, as are you."

He still had not denied the truth of the tale. "Are we more civilized? Tell me, Thor, my old friend: how does it feel to still walk in the shadow of Baldr and to hear him always called *the best* and yet know he would have betrayed all of you -- all of us -- if he'd had the chance? How does it feel to never measure up to him and always know you will be the lesser brother to a traitor who didn't give a damn?"

Thor's hand moved, a blade glittering in the faint light. Loki expected the knife to come his way like the goblet, but instead Thor drove the blade into the wood of the table. He glared at having the old tale undone now. Ah, but wasn't he the hero? Wasn't he the one who saved them from the treachery, though Loki had paid the price for what had happened?

"And you, Vali, now you know your father knew what you had done and he left you the forgotten son . . . the one he never could trust you afterwards. Isn't that so, Odin? Thor was devious enough for you. Thor did what was right. But Vali did what others would have thought of *me*. *Would you know yet more?*"

"Enough, Loki," Odin warned, his voice going ominous. The room chilled and frost formed on goblets. "We have heard all we need to."

Had he finally hit a nerve? Oh, but he wasn't done. Not yet.

"Have you? Where is Baldr now? Where is the *best of us all* while we go against the Chinese? Why, in fact did the Chinese choose us as their adversaries? Why not the Greeks? Why not the Romans?"

"They wanted Frigg and her ability to see the fates of people," Odin replied.

"Sybil could have done the same. Why Frigg? How did they get hold of her?" Loki looked Odin in the face and dared the murderous glare. They had the attention of everyone again. "*Where is Baldr?*"

"He's with the Chinese, of course," Odin finally replied. The glare disappeared amid another rush of whispers. He didn't look as bothered as he had a moment before. Maybe Loki had done him a favor by bringing the truth out now so Odin didn't have to announce this problem later, before the battle. The thought almost amused him. "What does it matter?"

"It matters to *me* what lies you tell this time. I will not be taking the blame this round, Odin. Not to protect you and your legends."

"Why worry? None of us may survive this time. The Chinese have Frigg. They have Baldr. They came for you." He leaned forward this time and stared at Loki. "Tell me you were not leading us into a trap there at the station."

"I didn't --" He stopped as another thought occurred to him. "So, you were the one put the knife in my back and that's the reason the Valkyrie thought I wouldn't be safe with you."

"Simply to stop you. I didn't kill you, but I didn't trust you, either."

"My, just like old times, isn't it?" He sat and lifted his goblet, the gold icy cold beneath his fingers. "I did not plan to be here, and quite honestly, I don't care if the Chinese take out the lot of you, but I have never been a traitor. I have always remembered another old saying: *If evil thou knowest, as evil proclaim it. And make no friendship with foes.*"

Odin nodded agreement.

And they went back to the feast.

CHAPTER THIRTEEN

Sounds grew louder. Closer . . . strident, bothersome creatures daring to approach him. They moved through the emptiness encased in their own coverings of magic, a mockery of this shell he had dwelled within for an eternity. P'an Ku stretched. Colors swirled and grew and spread out around him, drawing his attention for a moment. Or for days. He had no sense of time and so no need of it.

However, the others continued to move closer, coming for some purpose. Their annihilation would be the end result, no matter what they thought they sought. He would wipe everything away. The nearest first, because they were too close and loud. Then others he sensed, spread out everywhere, making their incessant noises.

Cleanse everything. Start something new.

But . . . he had been a long time alone and asleep, barely aware of anything beyond his shell. A part of him began to understand the concept of loneliness, an infection that came from the others. He could have banished the feeling with a thought, but held on instead. Something different to experience. Something odd and empty. He tested the feeling out, seeking more among the others. There, one sitting alone, wishing to be with others, fearing the future. He shared a moment with the woman and moved on, savoring the emotions.

So he waited a while longer.   After all, he could destroy them at any time with a thought.

But not quite yet.

CHAPTER FOURTEEN

S omewhere not far away, Frigg sensed the presence of her usual companions. She could almost look in on them and knew they feasted this night. Oh yes, Odin wouldn't miss such an opportunity to bring them together and add power to the myth.

She would have enjoyed being there tonight rather than sitting in this cold, shapeless room, waiting to throw the runes and read future paths, all of which became increasingly chaotic with each throw. Things were going to happen. She could feel the movements more clearly than she had felt anything in a long time. The future actions and changes centered, not surprisingly, around Loki.

P'an Ku moved, a surge of power, color and intent. He focused on her for a terrifying heartbeat before he looked elsewhere. Her hands trembled in the aftermath of that gaze. She tried to block out everything but here and now. She didn't want to see beyond this room.

Something else intruded; dark, formless and dangerous in ways she couldn't name. She sat still in the awful presence, knowing this to be something outside her understanding and far more dangerous than P'an Ku in his own way. But whatever was there pulled aside as though as uncertain of her as she was of it. Relief filled her and she let out a strangled sob. Whatever she kept touching was a problem for the future. She had felt this presence before, had a feel for trouble somewhere in the future, but only if they survived this current problem. She couldn't say if they would.

She had to hope for the best as she had always done. Was this too late to question her choices? She had seen things, though -- things outside the norm. Two paths spread out in front of them and one led to emptiness. She feared the dark, endless abyss. She feared the time when humanity would be gone and maybe the Gods with them. What should they want? What should they do?

Chu Jong was a pretentious, self-serving bastard and, unfortunately, the future seemed to be in his hands. She would have wished differently. She would have dared kill him herself, if she hadn't known that future led to disaster as well.

Yes, there were things worse than the dark abyss. She had, for one moment, glimpsed a future of endless torment, of everyone caught in a web and fed to a great power who did not care except to draw more power from the life he destroyed. She had thought the destruction came from Chu Jong at first, but now realized this happened if Chu Jong was removed from the picture before anyone else might step in and take his place.

So she had to let him play along the edge of the abyss and but now she worried Loki might be the one to push them all in.

She threw the runes again.

CHAPTER FIFTEEN

C hu Jong charted the course through the bright stars. He hated this place, with the bits and pieces of settlements, the scattering of humans, all untidy and haphazard. Nothing tied them together here; nothing brought them to kneel before the Gods as they should.

The scattering of humans, all going their own way, mocked the Gods and everything holy.

He could feel the whisper of power calling to him. Draco they called this area. Dragon. While the humans fled in panic, the *Imperial* went onward, seeking glory. He stared ahead, catching the first glimmer of power so strong and real a mere glimpse warmed him even at a distance.

"Sir," someone said. "The area ahead of us is extremely unstable. Perhaps we should pull away --"

He spun, anger growing at the interruption of his thoughts. How dare this human question him! He almost reached out and scattered the essence of the creature to the stars and beyond so that this insect never again linked a single molecule-to-molecule.

The creature took a step backwards, paling before such rage. A breath came to Chu Jong. Not creature . . . this was a being only a step away from Godhood; immortal, devoted. . . . Chu Jong frowned, though not so much at the man as at himself. His reaction had been overwrought. He prided himself on his calm, rational thinking.

The mere touch of power from the region ahead had lifted him into another realm. He had despised the humans and resented their intrusion. Was this what it meant to be a greater God? Had he touched upon his destiny at last?

"We go on," he said, calm returned. "We go on to what we are destined to be and glory awaits there that none could imagine."

He did not say the glory would be *theirs*. The others returned to their work, content to go where he bade them, as was their duty. He should have punished the fool who dared to question . . . but he let the affront go this time. This was the weakness of human thoughts still clinging to the immortal body, the weakness of one who had been born a man and never knew enough to cast off those chains.

Did none but Chu Jong see beyond the limitations of human life? Did anyone else seek out a greater existence?

He looked towards the Draco stars and the place where P'an Ku awoke. Chu Jong smiled for the future, free of fools and those who dared question him. He left the control room, changed his black and red suit for silken robes, and hurried to his rooms to prepare for the future.

For *his* future.

CHAPTER SIXTEEN

The feast had not been what Torin expected.

The moment Koil rose and said he had a tale to tell, Torin looked for weapons to be drawn. He had the laser in the holster under his arm, but he didn't want to use the weapon here, uncertain of how the technology would react in this place filled with so much magic. Koil and computers didn't get along; a whole room filled with Norse Gods? No, the laser was not the weapon he would want to use.

"Well, this is going to be interesting," Fenrir said.

Not at ease. Not the way his eyes flickered from right to left, measuring enemies, which didn't help Torin's state of mind. He decided to keep track of Fenrir as the best guide to know where to spot the danger.

Koil told his tale. The room grew tense. People shouted. People denied.

Odin did not.

By the end, Torin suspected he had drunk too much mead and would have enjoyed a fight anyway. Maybe this had always been part of the problem. He was blood of these people and their myths were filled with battles and war and he had never taken part in any of them. He hadn't been there for the Twilight of the Gods or the Doom of the Gods.

Fenrir and Hel took him to his room. Tyr gave a friendly enough nod in the hall, though he didn't come closer to them, which worried Torin at first until he recalled how Tyr and Fenrir had a problem, considering the wolf had bit off Tyr's hand.

He glanced at Fenrir and tried not to shudder.

Just as well they took him to his suite. On a normal ship he could have found his way, but not here. The damned place changed, the paths curving and moving as he watched, which was not good for someone with too much mead in his system. He would not get ill. He used a little magic to clear away some of the effects and took a deeper breath of the crisp, cool air, so sweet he thought the air must have blown down from some distant mountain and should not have been part of a ship's system. Was this a taste of Earth?

The wall colors had changed. Torin saw a line of dark black and red running along the shifting surface and shook his head. "That doesn't look good."

Fenrir nodded. "Too many dark emotions today. Loki set things in action. But the truth is known now, which will make a difference."

"A good difference," Hel added as they reached Torin's room. He welcomed them in with a wave of his hand and closed the door behind Hel. He was glad for the chance to talk to them now, in private. But how private? Who could hear?

Did it matter?

"Why do you think this is better?" he asked as they settled in the chairs by the desk.

"They expected Loki to betray them," Fenrir replied, anger flashing in his amber eyes and his hands curling around the arms of the chair. "They expected, at the very least, for Thor to try to kill him for having killed Baldr. Now the others know the truth, which makes a difference in how the rest of this plays out. We don't need the old lies to come between anyone and their good sense."

"But they don't trust him."

"They never did," Fenrir explained with a wry smile. "But

they don't trust each other, either. And now they are going to wonder what other lies Odin has let fall unremarked."

"There won't be much time to get any real grudges going," Hel added and tilted her head, listening to a filmy shape whispering at her ear. It moved away, went through the walls without pause, confirming Torin's thoughts about privacy. "We are near the area of disturbance and will soon go to battle against the Chinese. Despite all the anger, distrust and dislike growing over the eons, the Norse will stand together and they will not be looking for treachery from Loki, so no one is going to try and kill him before the true battle. This is good. We need Loki."

"So we can all fall together?" Fenrir asked.

"If we fall, everything falls," Hel answered with a wave of her hand, scattering spirits. "You know this, right, Torin? This is not some little *Ragnarok*. We are facing a God who can wipe out the universe and start over, if P'an Ku decides he doesn't accept what he finds."

"That doesn't seem possible," Torin admitted and quelled the shiver trying to take hold of him. He'd not felt the true fear until this moment, looking into her face. "I know the truth and understand on a mythic level, but I've lived too long in the modern human world. I've studied science and I know about novas and supernovas . . . and I can't get around this concept and accept what we're heading for as anything but natural."

They looked at him as though he had been talking another language. He'd never realized the gulf until then.

"Why does P'an Ku have this power?" he suddenly asked.

They stared, frowning as though they didn't know what he asked. He might as well be saying, 'why do you breathe?' for all the reaction he got.

"Not even Odin could do what P'an Ku might." He leaned forward, trying to break through the wall marking him as different from all the others. "He's a God and don't the Gods need the belief of the humans to stay strong?"

"Not the First Gods," Hel said and shook her head. "They existed before humans, before the other Gods, before anything. We are calling this one P'an Ku because the Chinese are influencing . . . everything, including us. What we perceive as this Elder God might be perceived entirely different if we were following the Greeks in. But whatever this being is, he is something from before belief existed."

"How can we hope to stop him?"

"I don't know," Hel admitted. She listened for a moment to a whisper at her ear and then another. She frowned. Odd, Torin thought, how he had gotten used to her companions. "The Chinese have the upper hand. Odin might have a better idea of what to do, but, somehow, I suspect much of this is going to come together when we face the trouble."

"He wanted Loki," Fenrir replied with several blinks of his large, amber eyes. "So did the Chinese. I think. . . ."

"Chaos," Torin said and nodded. "Yes, there might be something in chaos that can help us."

They both nodded and stood, ready to go. Fenrir stopped at the door and looked at him. "This is going to be interesting. But I would have rather met you at a calmer time."

They left. Torin thought it odd how the wolf was unsettled by this situation. He was not going to rest well tonight.

CHAPTER SEVENTEEN

This was not a day to listen to the *barbarian* prattle and make demands. Chu Jong had suffered through enough such sessions already. He brushed his fingers through the silken white beard he had decided to grow that afternoon to create the vision of an ancient sage. Would a sage listen to this drivel? Now was the time to take charge and show this fool he had no real power here.

"I demand to know what you plan next." Baldr leaned forward, his blond hair hanging in strands, unkempt as the rest of him. How could this thing pretend to be a God, let alone be a civilized one? Chu Jong saw madness in those eyes, far more obvious than when they had first met. "I must know what is going on so I can plan best how to deal with the Norse."

"To deal with your people," he replied feeling a little needle of irritation.

"I left them. They are not like me."

So true. I suspect they might still understand honor, he thought. He didn't say the words aloud.

"I must know --"

"Come with me." Chu Jong brushed away the dirt of this place. He hated this room and this creature, useful though Baldr had been to his plans. Baldr had given him many keys to use against the Norse and if Chu Jong hadn't thought there might be a key or two more, he would have been tempted to be done with this thing and destroy him; a gift to his sanity and even a gift to the Norse. He could be magnanimous as he neared perfection -- but not to this creature. "Come."

Baldr hated taking even simple orders, but the abhorrence fought with the knowledge he would get no answers if he remained behind. So he followed Chu Jong to the door and out of the rooms where he had stayed for so long.

Plainly, stepping outside of the little cell made Baldr uncomfortable. They didn't go far through the frost and scattering of snow gathering in piles against the walls. The climate changed somewhat at the next curve; a little better here than in the cold and dark of Baldr's self-created world, which said something more about his state of mind.

Chu Jong pushed open the door and entered first. The woman sat behind her table with the runes, as ever, spread before her. He thought she might spend her time doing nothing but read them.

Baldr followed him in . . . and stopped, horror crossing his face, which was not the reaction Chu Jong had expected. He detested surprises; they upset the symmetry of his plans. He had expected Baldr to be surprised, but not afraid.

"Frigg," Baldr whispered, staring at the woman. He took a step backwards, as though to flee, before he remembered Chu Jong. His face regained color from the snow white of a moment before. "What -- what is she doing here? She's dangerous! Odin will come for her --"

"Of course he will. He already follows. Did you think he followed to get you away from us? We needed a true prize for him to gain."

The stab went true. Baldr's eyes showed anger and distrust. No matter. Chu Jong found Frigg far more interesting to watch. She observed the interaction with a little play of a smile at her pale lips, as though the scene pleased her. Strange woman. She didn't seem to fear being here. What did she see in those runes?

So far, she had told him nothing.

"You don't understand about Frigg." Baldr looked as though he was prepared to run and escape. "She's powerful and dangerous in ways you can't control."

"But have you not told me the Norse are barbaric and weak? And yet you fear this *woman*?" He found the situation amusing. "You came to me with such words, remember. Should I now think you lied, Baldr? What should I fear? She's not *my* Goddess."

Frigg looked up and smiled, though Chu Jong thought there might be more madness than joy in her icy stare. "*Of the deeds ye two of old have done, Ye should make no speech among men; Whate'er ye have done in days gone by, Old tales should ne'er be told.*"

Chu Jong felt as though he watched someone come awake from a deep sleep. He felt a whisper of power he had not noticed before and when her hands moved over the runes and they danced without her touching them . . . he didn't want to know what she saw there.

Baldr's breath caught as the woman focused on him.

"*Baldr lives in the land I know that lies so fair, and from evil fate is free,*" she said. Her blue eyes narrowed to pebbles of frozen water. "But you can't go home, can you? You never could. Do you think I wouldn't know what you did, all those eons past? Do you think I wasn't aware of your treachery?"

"You wept at my death," Baldr whispered. "You did. You and all the others except --"

"I didn't weep for *you*. I wept for the outsider, for the one the others would capture in their wrath, because they could never accept such evil and treachery in one of their own."

"You wept for *Loki*? For him and not for me? Though I was dead and banished -- so long, so long in the dark, alone and abandoned and none to call me back."

"You did not deserve to come back."

"How can you --"

"Loki suffered, but you only died -- and you died none too soon. They blamed Loki, but you were the one who set the evil in motion. You brought us to *Ragnarok* when you first went with your tail between your legs, begging for scraps from the Roman table. When the Romans lost you, it was already too late. The cold had come upon us and we had no escape from the wicked deeds you set in motion."

Chu Jong realized he had been a fool.

He had never considered how Baldr might be repeating his own mythic past when he came to the Chinese. He had thought this destiny when the barbarian came to him just when he began looking for such a scapegoat to show to P'an Ku. Who had set this game in motion?

"You knew and yet you said nothing to the others," Baldr replied, making the words into an accusation. "You let them torture Loki."

"It has never been my place to manipulate, only to see. You can't know the pain doing nothing cost me. However, the past is done. You wouldn't repeat the same mistake, would you?"

She looked at Chu Jong. Until now, she had been a mad woman who spouted nonsense in her rune-readings. Now . . . now he felt as though he had been manipulated. He began to wonder who was casting the *I Ching*; who now read the turtle shell and dictated his life? Frigg was more than a sideshow in this play. He had not been paying attention.

"Shall I tell you your fate, Chu Jong?"

"You are not my Goddess," he repeated and forced himself to believe those words. Her runes meant nothing to him.

"We are all first children of the Earth; we are all linked. Haven't you figured this out yet? You think you can control such a being as P'an Ku? You think by showing him an exterior form you can hide what is in the heart?"

He did *not* want to hear such words and refused to believe

the implications. He backed away and Baldr went with him. Chu Jong pulled the door closed, but not before he heard her mocking laughter. They left, remaining silent all the way to Baldr's room where the barbarian entered, quiet and undemanding at last.

Chu Jong walked away, his fingers brushing against the silk of his clothing and the sage beard he had grown, but the movements were too nervous. He wanted away from the Norse, both of them . . . but he feared their cold had spread and he walked a long ways to his own safe place.

CHAPTER EIGHTEEN

L oki left the feast not long after he told his tale. The others had grown more boisterous again, but a hint of anger hung in the air, mingled with distrust -- but not disbelief. They didn't like him any better for having told the truth, though.

The Valkyrie went with him, a very noble and frightening bodyguard. He had to trust them. Torin watched him leave with one eyebrow raised and with a slight shake of his head. He sat with Fenrir and Hel still; he'd be safe with Loki's two most famous children.

He would have trusted Frigg to protect them both. He would go through the rest of this madness for her. He would get her back, although not for any of the rest of this group. They meant nothing to him.

Oh, he lied to himself with those thoughts. He knew it. They meant pain and old wounds and long smoldering fires of hatred and vengeance. However, he'd unexpectedly lost much of his old desire for revenge when he took in Torin and raised him. He had stopped hunting for the Norse and listening for rumors, which was why they had caught him so much by surprise at the station and *Chaos*.

"Do I need your protection still?" he asked, looking to Skuld who walked beside him.

"Do you think you made friends with your old tale of

truths?" she asked, giving an unexpected snort of amusement.
"You may have released Thor from an old lie burning in his
soul, and perhaps Vali as well, but now the others are looking at
Odin and wondering what other things he concealed from them
for oh-so-long. And some are thinking they would rather not
have known the truth and seen a legend ruined."

"So I was unwise."

"No." She slowed and looked at him differently than
before, a hint of awkwardness almost hidden. "We did not know
the truth, either, Loki."

"And yet you took me in, though you thought I had
murdered Baldr?"

"Murder, war, battles. . . ." She shook her head. "We don't
judge as others do. Or perhaps we sensed more in you. And
Frigg never spoke badly of you. I think . . . she knew?"

The idea bothered him. Had Frigg known the truth and
done nothing to help him? Loki didn't want to believe so, but
the thought drove a little dagger into his heart with a pain he
hadn't known he could still feel. *Betrayal?* Oh, he should have
been long past such a feeling.

They said nothing more the rest of the way to their odd
little world-within-a-world. Skuld led him to a room and
nodded for him to go inside while two Valkyrie took the guard
posts outside the door.

He went to the bed and sat. Tired. Very tired. This was a
weariness more of the soul than of the body. He shouldn't have
been here. This was not his war. And if Frigg had betrayed him
as well, why should he care what happened to her now?

No. No, he had to think past this anger. He had to
remember other times. Talking to Frigg . . . she had spoken
with him often, much to the consternation of Odin. He
thought maybe she had done so to annoy her husband. Now he
wondered if she didn't care. If so, what did she care about?

He rested, fully clothed, except to kick off his boots. He

wasn't going to relax in this ship. He wasn't going to. . . .

Sleep and dream? Oh, yes, the dream took him suddenly. He almost fought the scene away before he recognized the place and the time; the wooded glade, a remembrance so strong that in the dream he could smell the pine, taste the hint of smoke on the air and feel the snow falling against his face. He recalled this time and place and knew -- yes, there came Frigg.

"Lady," he had said, always so polite with her. He had done her mischief once upon a time and regretted the prank ever since. He had wanted to know if she would foresee his plan to cut off her hair. Maybe she had known and let him do so anyway and won the gold of the dwarves for it. Maybe she had manipulated him to the action.

He had always wondered but he had never asked questions of her.

"Loki," she replied, her words soft and floating on the winds of time. She moved, ghost-like, to stand before him, her icy eyes staring into his soul while her hair, grown long and wild since his old prank, flew about on the wind. The stare came clearly while everything around them became unfocused. He remembered the moment with a heart-pounding clarity overcoming the eons that had passed. "The woods are growing darker," she whispered and touched the side of his face. "So much will change."

He'd hated to hear those words, even then. "Change? Nothing changes here."

"You will survive. You will be wiser for what happens. The others . . . they will cling too much to what they are. You will be the better of those who feast at Valhalla in the end."

"Loki the Prankster?"

"I can see behind the mask. I can see all the secrets."

But he'd had no secrets then. Not really. Probably she had meant the secrets others tried to keep from her. He hadn't considered such a thing, then. Now --

He came awake remembering the look on her face and the weight of her sorrow. He had wanted to cheer her up. He had planned to do something silly, but Thor asked him to secretly take a message to his people, the Risi. And he'd gone. He and Thor had grown apart of late, but they had been close as brothers once and *he* still felt the bond.

Gods, the memory of Thor's treason hurt sometimes. He hadn't expected the agony now when he had finally shed his rage. He slowly stood and began to pace the pain out of him. He wanted this madness to finally end. He wanted to be done and finished with the Norse and their lies and if that meant they all went to chaos, so be it. Start over. Forget everything and hope for something better the next time around.

He couldn't. He couldn't because --

Because Frigg was *right*. He had survived and he was wiser and he wouldn't forget there were more than Gods at stakes in this battle. He had human friends who would be lost and never come back. They lived too short a life already; he would not purposely do something to end their existence faster. He should have listened to Frigg more often in those old days. But, back then, he didn't think anything would ever change. They had their daily dramas; they had their nightly feasts. The battles came and went; the worthy were saved to fight again.

Was this what they had become? The worthy chosen to go the battle once more?

He would help get Frigg free and this time he would ask her.

CHAPTER NINETEEN

Others bowed when Chu Jong passed, all the minor deities and the near-mortals who served him showing their respect. No tiger followed him; they saw his greatness alone. He found their belief a comfort and hoped they didn't see the doubt in him. The feeling had come, unexpectedly, after he left the crazy Northern Witch. The seed she had planted had entangled treacherous vines with the Queen of the West's conversation and both had taken root in his heart after he left the shaken Baldr in his icy room.

This was not what he planned. His vision had been faultless, symmetrical in all the beauty of perfection, with everything falling into place --

Laugher, high-pitched and unnatural, shook him from his thoughts. He found Monkey King hanging from one of the silken curtains. With a laugh, the creature dropped, becoming less animal-like as he moved, growing taller so he looked Chu Jong in the face. Monkey King might be able to *ape* the ability to appear the same as the rest of them, but there was always a bit of monkey in him, curious and irreverent to all the true Gods believed. They should never have brought this one into the heavens.

"Oh, not happy, our Chu Jong, our arbiter of the heavens, the one who has decided all our fates? Is this not right? Is the plan not as good as one thought, oh great and mighty Chu Jong? Could it be you lack understanding?"

"I understand well enough," he answered with a snarl and started to step past. Monkey King moved into his path, an inane smile on his lips. "I have work."

"Oh yes. Important work to march through the halls and watch all bow in supplication to the *Great One.* Oh, but I have not, have I? How could I be so blind?" And he bowed so mockingly that the very act put Chu Jong's teeth on edge.

"What do you want?" he demanded finally.

"Oh, you know. The usual. Peaches, fine wine, women. . . ." The smile left his face. "Not to have to deal with fools."

"Are you calling me a fool?" Chu Jong's hand moved to the knife he carried, hidden in his robes.

"If you pull your knife, you'll be wearing the blade through your heart," Monkey King answered. No humor showed in his face. "And then where will all your fine plans be?"

"You mock me."

"I mock everyone. It is my nature."

"Leave me alone. I have --"

"Work to do. Oh, yes."

Chu Jong snarled and pushed past Monkey King, as little as he liked to touch the creature. He took a dozen steps, listening carefully, but the thing was not following him, at least.

"I was born from a stone left behind from P'an Ku's own shell when he created the world," Monkey King shouted behind him. "And you *are* a fool."

Chu Jong spun and saw little more than the shadow of Monkey King leaping up the wall, swinging across the silks and disappearing. He had been, in fact, a twice-damned fool. He had dismissed Monkey King as nothing of importance long before they left Earth; had dismissed and forgotten everything about the creature and now found a link he could have exploited.

This was not going the way he had planned.

CHAPTER TWENTY

L oki felt an odd tug at his mind as he came awake, aware of power beyond the walls of *Asgard* where strands of chaos drifted through space, tickling the hull of the ship with possibilities unrealized. The room seemed to blaze with colors and he felt a tingle of anticipation as he waved a hand to clean his clothing and prepare . . . for something. He already waited at the door when Freyja arrived. With a silent nod, he followed her out of the lair of the Valkyrie, suspecting he would never return to the odd place. This had been an unusual experience, but he hadn't rested well while here.

The halls felt peculiar today and he watched the surface of the walls swirling with too many colors and the patterns changing too often. Loki suspected there were a lot of worried Gods waking to the feel of things out of place and touch power they had not felt since a battle long ago.

He and Freyja went to the control deck where she nodded and stepped aside, staying as a visible guard inside the door. Torin arrived a dozen heartbeats later and they both stared at the miasmic confluence of light and power sweeping across the star-studded sky.

"Well, that looks like trouble," Torin said.

Which won a chuckle from Loki. He lifted his hand -- funny to see how some of the others tensed -- and felt out the lines before them. "This area is ready to explode. Literally.

We'll have a super-nova here and the destruction will spread farther than the humans would guess. Sun after sun is going to go when this one does. It would be glorious to see, if any of us would survive."

"And you think we can somehow stop a star from going nova?" Torin asked, startled and worried for the first time.

"The heart of the star is the Chinese God awakening inside his shell. He'll cast the covering off and start the process. We need only convince him not to wake, right?"

"This sounds worse and worse," Torin mumbled.

Oddly, Thor was the one who nodded agreement. He looked more furtive than angry today and Loki could see less tension in the lines of his face and the set of his shoulders. Damn. Maybe having the truth finally told was not such a painful experience for him, which would be Loki's sort of luck, doing Thor a favor after all this time, when he had meant to strike a blow.

Sometimes there was no winning.

"There is a world on the edge of this mess," Odin reported as he left one of the stations. Interesting to see how he had taken the time to learn anything about ships and technology. "And the world is where the Chinese have gone to ground, ship and all."

"We might have a chance of taking them if we can get there fast enough," Tyr added. He read over some computer screens, updating information on the main screen, the words dancing up and down along the edges. So, the Norse were not so tech blind as some pantheons Loki had seen.

Loki had expected the Norse to be worse for some reason, but that had probably been his own bigotry. They were not as ancient as many of the other groups, which might have helped them move forward with less trouble. And they did not have Loki's trouble with computers, which came more from his link to chaos than his place in the Norse pantheon.

"If we try to land, I don't think we'll surprise them much." Loki read the reports, analyzing information and keeping tight hold on his own emotions. "They know we followed them. They would have an advantage, watching us land. But we can't attack from here, either with magic or technology. They have too strong a shield."

"True. We could take shuttles, which would make good target practice for them," Tyr added with a wave of his gloved hand. Bionic? "Should we go straight for P'an Ku?"

"No," Loki and Odin choroused, which amused everyone.

"Not a good idea then," Tyr agreed with a laugh. How odd; this felt natural, being here. Even Thor's perpetual frown had disappeared.

"I can get us there in a way they won't expect," Odin said. He lifted a hand and magic shimmered in his fingers with a sparkling of tiny stars. "We need to get close before they see us."

"And we will get there how?" Thor asked.

"Oh, by an old, *old* road."

A few minutes later they were leaving *Asgard*.

Loki felt a surge of wonder when he saw Bifrost again, the bright rainbow bridge brought to life at a wave of Odin's hand, eons past, and light-years away, from where the magical road had last stood. He knelt and brushed his hand against the shimmering surface, basking in the feel of such power stretching out beyond the airlock. Of everything that had survived *Ragnarok*, this had been the most beautiful.

"It won't disappear," Odin said with a breathless laugh.

So, not so easy to do, this powerful magic. Loki hid his own pleasure at the sight of the bridge. After all, he was not really one of them. The outsider, the adopted one -- he did not have the same claim to this power as the others.

Oh, but closer to them than *anything* else alive now.

There was an odd and frightening thought. He looked

around for Torin and found him with Fenrir and Hel, all three of them nearby. Others began pouring out of Valhalla: the worthy ready to do battle again. He hadn't realized there would be so many and shivered to see them stand with axes, swords and shields in hand. He wanted to order Torin back, but he couldn't. Torin was late to the bloodline and myths, but he had been born part of them as well.

Odin started out first, Thor at his side with Mjolnir glowing in his hand. Loki let them go a few steps ahead before he followed. He didn't trust Thor at his at his back. Torin moved to Loki's side. He didn't want the boy this close to the front --

"Don't say it," Torin warned with a tap on Loki's arm. "I'm not a child."

Loki gave a sigh and nodded. Maybe this was better. He could protect Torin if he could keep him in sight. He cast a worried look at Fenrir and Hel, following behind them. Shouldn't he be as worried about protecting those two? They were his true children. Had he lost track of who he was and what was important?

He had never doubted so much the last time they went to battle.

The path lead downward through empty space, a magical shell arching over the rainbow bridge. He could see only tiny spots of magical light playing around them as they moved forward. The Chinese had put a shell of magic around the world, protecting them from the storm raging in the heavens nearby, though Loki doubted the magic would hold for long -- another reason to be done with this quickly. The Norse pressed forward at inhuman speeds, down into the thermosphere, mesosphere and stratosphere where they stopped for a moment above the clouds. Cold here and if they had been human, they wouldn't have survived even with the protective magic of Bifrost around them . . . but this moment brought Loki back to his true self again. The call of battle sounded in the thunder below and when Odin started out again, Loki wasn't slow to follow.

They raced through rain-drenched clouds, the wind swirling around them with the icy cold of home. Lightning flashed close by and thunder roared. He couldn't tell if the storm came from them or the Chinese, or maybe from nature. All three perhaps; they created a disturbance here, the Chinese and the Norse, and nature would react to the intrusion of so much magic.

Once past the clouds, he could see sharp mountains and wide valleys, verdant with growth and rich with streams. A huge building with red roof and angular walls sat below and he sensed the essence of the Chinese ship, *Imperial*. There was the storehouse of their power, nestled close to the world.

Loki began to see the enemy in their perfect lines, red and black uniforms resplendent against the almost unnatural green of the field where they waited, protecting the large building which had been their ship. The Chinese had brought out the dragon, Tialong's serpentine body twisting with agitation. The Norse were ready this time. Odin rushed forward with a battle cry and others swarmed past Loki with joyous shouts of their own.

They had all been too long from the battle. Even the Valkyrie rose into the air with cries of power and promises of glory as they swooped forward with the rest.

"Damn, that's impressive," Torin said, startled.

"It was always our . . . *their* way. The battle was the heart of their culture."

"*Our culture*. You are one of them. I can feel the call in my blood." Torin drew his laser. "I think it's safe enough to use my weapon of choice here, at least. Not so dangerous as in the ship."

Loki gave a nod of agreement, his attention on the battle -- the lovely, growing chaos -- below. Fenrir rushed past them, shifting from man to giant wolf as he moved, his shout of battle giving way to howl of challenge. Fenrir was the one who leapt at the dragon and they both tumbled away from the bridge. Fenrir howled and Tialong hissed, but they both landed, the ground shaking with the impact. Loki's heart pounded at the sight but he found himself diverted as one of the Chinese came from under the bridge and reached for him.

He kicked the bastard in the chest and sent him flying, too.

By the time he reached the ground, everyone battled in a tightly-packed group, friend and foe so close together he worried Odin might get behind him again with a blade. Oh yes, good friend and dangerous foe, and all alike to him.

He pulled his own knife and leapt into the attack with Torin at his side. They did well together amid the shouts, the cries and the never-forgotten scent of blood. Loki didn't have much trouble. He laughed, in fact, when he pulled a bit of chaos straight from the mass so close overhead and used the power to send enemies . . . somewhere else. He didn't know where they went. Maybe they'd all meet there if this didn't work.

He wasn't certain how they were going to stop P'an Ku from waking. No matter. One step at a time. At least this was glorious, dancing with death amidst the shouts, the cries and the last, surprised gasps before darkness took someone. This was the old world returned: glory and blood and --

They were wining. Not *Ragnarok*, this time. Not the final battle, the twilight of the Gods and the darkness afterwards. Good. He didn't want to spend centuries finding his way through the changes and changing to fit in again.

Here he could be himself once more.

Only . . . only a part of him whispered that the old Loki wasn't so great. The old Loki had been a barbarian, a trickster and someone who would have done those things they accused him of under different circumstances. He'd always detested Baldr. Maybe the others believed so easily in the lie because he had given them no reason to doubt.

Maybe his wishes and his chaos had led Thor to move against his brother.

He'd stopped to get his breath. He shouldn't think so much, not during battle. Torin remained at his side. Loki found a cut on his arm, but not serious and he didn't really feel any pain. Torin kept watch and the laser took out another enemy.

They were nearly to the side of a great, huge building, the walls growing taller and the building wider as he watched. No matter. Keep going. How many of these damned Chinese were there? He supposed a lot -- there always had been many of them. Maybe this had become part of their legend as well, which could make them damn harder to fight, with their endless stream of warriors.

He wasn't certain which of the Norse had fallen though he had seen the Valkyrie carrying away the bodies. Odin, Tyr and Thor led the others, forcing the battle onward with shouts that grew louder than the wind.

As they neared the building, Odin gave a shout of triumph and Thor echoed the sound. Fenrir and Tialong had backed away, taunting each other to attack again, their growls louder than the battle. They must have been well-matched. The others were starting to range around them, ready to go for the building --

The huge red doors opened and this time the Gods of the Chinese surged out in the forefront, a far more dangerous enemy than what they'd fought so far. No more time to think. Loki threw himself into the battle.

CHAPTER TWENTY-ONE

Chu Jong had watched the barbarians descend from the heavens on their pretty rainbow and leap into the attack without any thought. *Undisciplined.* He studied their movements while his array of warriors marched forward and engaged. These fools would be no match for his army. All he had to do was lure them in, let them fight their way to the building, wear themselves out and thin down their numbers. As they neared the Imperial Palace, Chu Jong smiled at the childishness of their attack and, with a wave of his arm, the doors opened and the Norse faced the true enemy.

He led the others out into battle and sent death with a wave of his hand. He cast destruction against the Norse Gods themselves and knew they could not stand before him.

Or so he thought at first.

The barbarians seemed none the worse for already having fought a battle. He would have thought they fed on blood and death if he hadn't studied them so carefully. The term berserker came to mind and he stared at them with a hint of worry for a moment. No, they hadn't changed into mindless beasts.

As he thought those words, a huge wolf appeared out of nowhere and leapt in among the soldiers and Gods, scattering the others and breaking the perfect pattern. Chu Jong yelled and raised his hand, intending to banish the creature. The amber eyes burned with hatred and dagger-sharp teeth snapped as the wolf leapt forward. Chu Jong pulled away in haste, fearing he would lose his hand to those brutal teeth.

Claws scored long furrows along his arm and fetid breath brushed across his face as the thing went for his neck. Chu Jong nearly panicked, but he shoved the creature away with an unnaturally strong force. The wolf flew sideways and impacted with the building, sliding into a boneless heap. Not dead, though. He got ready for the death blow --

Sharp pain burnt his arm, like lightning loosed against him. Someone had dared use a modern weapon, here on this sacred ground! He turned from the unmoving wolf, trying to find the new enemy in the mass of barbarians. There! Not even a full God, but some half-breed thing who dared to move against him. He banished the pain of both the burn and the other wounds, though the work took power. Another barbarian had stepped closer to the half-breed, this one a God of real power, brushing away his first attack with a smirk. Someone --

Oh yes, this was the one he wanted. *Truly wanted.* He had not expected Loki to come to the battle. He had thought Loki and the others were not on terms these days and yet there he stood, weapon in hand (How barbaric!) and fighting beside Odin himself. How had he misjudged them? Had Baldr lied to him about Loki?

No matter. He gave his orders. The others fell in around him and together they moved to capture the prize.

Once he controlled chaos itself, nothing could destroy his perfection.

CHAPTER TWENTY-TWO

L oki looked up as the entire focus of the Chinese warriors changed and they turned as one towards Torin and him. In a moment, they started forward. "Oh hell."

Torin had really annoyed the damned fat bastard. Whatever God he was -- the Chinese had so many -- he had more power over the others than Loki had expected. Loki appreciated what Torin had done, though. He would have regretted Fenrir going to the abyss and the long time before he could ever return -- unless one of the Valkyrie caught him up. He didn't think that would happen, though. He would never expect one of his children to be among those chosen any more than he would have been.

The Chinese were moving in on them now.

"Torin, get back. We need to get with Odin and the others. This guy is really pissed."

"Yeah. Sorry."

"No reason to be." Loki put a hand on Torin's shoulder and smiled as they backed away by several steps. "You did the right thing. Thank you."

Loki remained partly in front of him, but Torin kept the laser ready, aiming at the line of red and black uniforms. He dared a glance at the others. They weren't slow to come to help, though he didn't think their actions came from any personal love, of course. They were anxious to rejoin the fight and the battle was moving in his direction.

He was anxious as well, to be honest. So much so, he dared linger in front of the others. Waited and dared --

Loki hadn't thought they were coming for *him*. Stupid thing not to consider, knowing they'd tried to lure him out when they were on the station. He knew his mistake the moment they sent the magic at him from a dozen Gods, all from different directions, though none of the magic meant to kill him.

The spells swept in, the colors curling into tight braids, and he felt as though he'd been caught in the midst of fire. The lines of magic crossed and re-crossed him, circling in so fine a net he couldn't move so much as a finger. He could barely see, his eyes tearing with pain and half-blinded by the bright magic. He saw Torin try to reach him. Odin and Thor shoved Torin back, but those two kept coming.

The magic the Chinese created began to drag him towards the building. He had the feeling he didn't want to go there.

Thor lifted Mjolnir and with a shout of defiance sent the weapon flying. Loki expected the hammer to sail his way and destroy the magic and him. However, the hammer flew over his head and struck amid the mass of Chinese instead. The power holding him lessened . . . but not enough.

They dragged him inside. The doors swung shut, trapping him within a huge room of gold, silver and silk. The magic died little by little, replaced by subtle powers, binding him so he could not move his arms still. He found himself kneeling before some of the Chinese.

To hell with that.

He surged up to his feet.

They knocked him down.

He got up and spat blood from his mouth, letting it fall on the pretty tile floor.

"I am not some human to grovel before you." He looked

into the face of the fat bastard Torin had shot and wished he had managed a head shot so Loki didn't have to face this one because he could see trouble in the beady eyes and the curl of the lips behind the wispy white beard.

"You are a barbarian," the man said. "God or no, you are not *our* equal."

And with a wave of his hand, the Chinese God sent him to his knees once more. Painfully this time. Loki gasped and cursed.

And he stood again. This was a test. He would not give up.

Not while he was conscious, at least.

And that didn't last for long.

CHAPTER TWENTY-THREE

"When did Loki get so incredibly *stupid*!" Thor shouted, his frustration so plain Torin stared. Thor, he realized, was truly worried.

As the Chinese ensnared and dragged Loki off, the Norse fought madly -- some gone berserk, in fact -- and those had been slow to retreat at Odin's orders. The Chinese had taken Loki inside, making immediate rescue impossible. Power radiated from the white and red building. The moment Loki slipped through the huge red doors, they snapped shut with a sound of thunder . . . and the building grew larger.

Not a good sign.

Odin kept conference with the Ravens, both of whom had their heads bowed, listening to something through electronics. Torin wished he could access the devices to know what they tried to find. The others held back, forming in a line and mumbling their curses rather than shouting defiance. They all knew the loss of Loki would be a danger to them.

Did any of them consider Loki a friend, though? Did any of them worry that these damned Chinese might kill him and send him to the abyss? When would they meet again? Would they? Torin had immortal blood but he might not live long enough to see Loki again and, if he died, he couldn't be certain he'd be reborn.

Now wasn't the time to think about his own future. He

took a step closer to Odin, but a firm hand caught his arm and he began to snarl . . . and faced Fenrir.

"Don't bother him now." Fenrir caught his arm and drew him away. Blood stained Fenrir's arm and side, but the wounds had already started to heal. He'd be ready for the battle when the time came. "Odin and the Ravens are working; they'll fix this."

"And if they don't?"

"Then you and I and Hel will do what we can. But, in the interest of honesty, if Odin can't correct this problem, I don't expect the three of us to do any better."

Fenrir didn't know how stubborn Torin could be. He'd gotten that more from his father than from Loki. He wanted to shove his way forward and beat his way into the building. He remained by Fenrir and said nothing, his head bowed, fighting for control. This battle wasn't something he could take on alone. His own magic was strong enough so he could withstand any but the strongest of the Chinese Gods. And he could be tricky; he had learned the art from Loki. Patience he'd acquired from Sigyn, who had put up with both of them for as long as he could remember.

Torin called all those pieces together and forced an overlay of calm. He moved willingly with Fenrir whom he expected would not try to keep him safe, even if Loki had given such instructions. They had made a connection of sorts, which he had not expected to make with anyone from *Asgard*. Together they went to Bifrost, Fenrir limping but keeping to his feet. They sat on the edge of the rainbow where power radiated around them in a protective shield, though he didn't think they were powerful enough to hold the Chinese at bay. The Chinese were ancient in ways that made the Norse look like newcomers. He hadn't considered how their older status might affect the balance. Everything was symbolic, though -- and while the Chinese had venerable age on their side, the Norse had youthful vigor on theirs.

Many of the Norse straggled back to the rainbow bridge. Some were badly wounded and a few remained on the field where the Valkyrie swept in and grabbed the dead, taking some to Valhalla and others on to Freyja's field. Those last would not return to the battle. He wondered if they would be glad to be done with the never-ending cycle.

Hel stood a bit to the side, the spirits around her more frantic than before. Who were those dead? He suspected a few might have come from the Chinese. Hel had her own myths which were not a part of the battlefield and the Valkyrie.

Torin looked to Odin, impatient -- and saw the Ravens returned to their ancient forms, the huge birds flying off in different directions.

"Damn," Fenrir mumbled. "I don't know what that means, but it can't be anything good. He is looking for information, is our *Alfater.*"

"I suspect Hel is as well, in her own way," Torin suggested.

Fenrir glanced towards his sister and gave a quick nod. "The dead see things differently than we do and they are often not so much help as I hope. We --"

The ground shook; everyone stopped, both Norse and Chinese. The world trembled again, more violently, and as the ground moved, the rocks seemed to moan in protest.

"Loki," Fenrir whispered, his face pale. "We need to get him out."

The trembling stopped. Torin could feel the pressure building in the air and the ground, as though two forces were poised on either side, ready to crush those who caught between.

When Torin looked up, a shot of red flashed across the sky and the sun pulsed.

Not good.

They were running out of time.

CHAPTER TWENTY-FOUR

L oki awoke in a dank, dark cell; the stone walls were too close and the stink of something dead filled the air so he tried not to breathe deeply. He moved very little; everything ached and opening his eyes hurt. He couldn't move his arms which were secured behind his back by a rope with enough magic of its own so he couldn't simply destroy it. He might get free if he could think his way around the magic, but this wasn't going to happen quickly. Damn them. Damn *himself* for being such a fool and falling to their hands. He should have been more careful.

Torin would attempt to rescue him which meant he had put the boy in worse danger while trying to protect him. Loki feared Torin wouldn't come return from death, being half-mortal. His stupidity might cause the loss of something he had come to love too well.

He hated despair.

Loki fought his way to his knees, which was difficult without the use of his arms, and pushed to his feet. The room seemed to move around him and he leaned sideways, his head to the wall, ignoring the feel of dampness and slime as best he could. His head ached so badly it was a wonder he could think at all.

They'd trapped him. He was helpless and might as well be mortal. Still, he smiled when the door opened because the smile clearly annoyed and worried the man who swaggered in.

"I am Chu Jong. I rule here."

"Do you really?" Oh, he hit a nerve with the simple jab, which meant Chu Jong's position wasn't as strong as the man wished. His face reddened. This one was very easily played.

"You are my prisoner."

He couldn't argue the point. He didn't ask why he was a prisoner and wouldn't have trusted Chu Jong's answer anyway. He also couldn't place the name among the pantheon of Gods.

Baldr came through the door.

If Loki hadn't been bound, he would have taken him, just with his hands. Instead, Loki straightened, taller than both of these fools. The bonds would not hold him forever and he had a very long, long memory . . . as well as considerable pent up anger that hadn't yet found the proper release.

"I told you he would be no trouble," Baldr said with a wave of his hand. Did no one look into this fool's face? Madness played in those haunted, icy eyes. "And now, truly, you get what you deserve, Loki."

"Deserve?" he asked, uncertain what Baldr meant. He wasn't prepared for these guessing games.

"For what you did to me --"

"Oh, no, not that." He pushed away from the wall and saw how Baldr almost took a step backwards. "You know better. The dead know the truth."

"Truth?" Chu Jong asked. He seemed to be enjoying the game and the disdain he felt for Loki appeared to double when he faced Baldr. So, no love lost between these allies. He couldn't say the lack of love surprised him; Baldr hadn't changed for the better.

"He knows I had nothing to do with his death and he knows his brother Thor arranged the murder and his shapeshifting brother Vali took my part."

"This isn't true," Baldr growled, taking a step closer to

strike him.

Loki kicked first, aiming at the groin and making certain the blow counted. Baldr went down with a howl that barely covered the amused snort from Chu Jong. Loki almost fell as well, but he managed to stay to his feet and meet Chu Jong's look with an even stare. The man was no fool. He stayed out of range.

Baldr crawled to the doorway and pulled himself to his feet, his faced white and his eyes too large and dark. "*And who will watch over you this time?*" he asked, his words an unpleasant growl. "No one will come for you."

A simple wave of Baldr's hand and the world changed. He hadn't expected his old companion to have so much power here in the realm of the Chinese. Probably his rage gave Baldr new strength because Loki heard Chu Jong make a sound of surprise.

Loki knew this place where he now found himself stretched out on a hard rock, helpless as more power held him in place. Shadows moved above him and something slithered into view; he focused on the face of the Skathi's serpent where the creature hung from the rocks above. The mouth opened and venom dropped --

Acid burnt across his face and, as he thrashed in pain, the world moved beneath him. Sigyn and the bowl were not here to save him. The world trembled with him as the fire burnt again . . . and again.

In a brief moment of sanity, he thought they could not hold him forever. Torin would find him. Torin wouldn't abandon him.

But neither would the serpent ever let him go.

CHAPTER TWENTY-FIVE

Chu Jong had taken Baldr -- a cursing and limping Baldr -- back to his dingy, cold little room. He had offered no sympathy and had barely managed not to laugh at the fool's discomfort. Oh, if he could have allied with Loki instead, how different things would be! There was a God with fire and determination, but alas, also of honor already given to others. Chu Jong hadn't expected to find such morality in the any of the Norse and especially not from Loki, given the tales told about him.

Ah, but how many of those tales were true if the murder of Baldr was not? Baldr knew the truth, of course. Chu Jong thought to berate him for such lies but in the end he simply wanted away from the fool and not to have to deal with him for a while.

He had, at least, removed Loki from the scene. A God so in touch with chaos had been a danger to his plans, who might have disrupted his perfection and make the Chinese look no better than the Norse in the face of P'an Ku's judgment. He would take no such chance.

The ground shook. Loki, tortured as much by memory as by Baldr's tricks, reverted to old powers. Chu Jong blocked the quakes off so they didn't spread and unsettle his work. A frigid wind blew through the hall with a spattering of snow against the wall, a sign of Baldr's rage seeping through the closed door.

Chu Jong banished the baleful influence back into Baldr's tiny room. He would have no power in Chu Jong's world.

Chu Jong had learned a good many important facts from this encounter with Loki. He thought about how best to use the information. He went to his own suite, with the perfect walls, the whisper of willows and cranes somewhere by a pond he could not quite see beyond an orchard of cherry trees which were always in bloom. The sounds and scents soothed him. He sat at his desk and he worked. The future rested in his hands.

He had beat aside the Norse and captured one of the key players. With a thought, he peered in on Loki, watching him flinch at each drop of venom. Crude. Barbaric . . . but as long as this sufficed to keep Loki's focus during the rest of the event, he would let Baldr play.

A flick of his fingers dismissed the vision. The Norse were still on-world. He could sense them as they walked on *his* ground and he heard every plan they made. *Fools.* He smiled and wrote orders to counter their childish little games.

Winning would be easier than he expected . . . and, being a wise God, he mistrusted the thought.

CHAPTER TWENTY-SIX

The next drop of venom did not burn his skin, nor the one after it, though he heard Skathi hiss and move. Loki took a shuddering breath of relief, despite the burning pain still spreading across his face. "Sigyn," he whispered and tried to see, but the venom blinded him.

"No, not she," someone replied; an odd voice but that might have been a reflection of the venom and pain. "But we are not enemies, either. Can you get him loose, Red?"

The lessening of pain combined with a dread of the next drop of venom hitting him. Loki felt almost giddy as he realized someone else worked strong magic to get him free. He tried to focus on what was going on, at least mentally, but connections were not coming.

"Luck is with us," someone said with a quiet laugh. "When the barbarian bound him to the rock, our fine Chu Jong let go of his own control. He won't know what we do."

"As long as we act quickly."

"Have faith, Monkey King. I am almost done here."

Something came free from his arms and legs. Hands caught Loki and pulled him away from the rock, moving quickly despite his moan of pain. He didn't ask his saviors to slow. He could see nothing but moving shadows, but he heard the hissing anger of the serpent. He feared the evil creature would come for them.

Should he trust these strangers?

He could barely move his arms and legs and only in painful twitches. Magic and venom had sapped his strength, leaving him vulnerable. After they had moved for a while, his eyes began to pick out smudges of colors as they reached . . . somewhere else. The air grew fetid and thick, humidity and temperature rising so fast he thought he couldn't breathe for a moment. He wanted the cool --

"No, no. Do not call your northern ice down upon us," Red warned. "They will know where you are for certain then. Be calm. You are safe."

"Am I?" His voice sounded hoarse. The wounds on his face, raw and bleeding, made talking painful. He would need time to heal them. And then. . . .

"Rest here," the other said. Monkey King. The name meant something to him and he realized why this one didn't sound entirely human. He thought they must have brought him to some jungle, created in the way Gods always created the places that appealed best to them. Power lurked everywhere around them. Loki pulled some of the magic closer, being careful as he healed wounds, making no show which might draw attention to them. He could breathe easier. He blinked and shapes began to come into focus.

"Thank you." He meant those words. He had feared an eternity of madness -- or had hoped for a quick end with the rebirth of P'an Ku and everything and everyone else be damned and lost, even those he loved. "Thank you, but why?"

"Because *we* are not fools," the man across from him replied. Red Coat -- God of Luck. He began to recall bits and pieces of what he'd learned about some of the Chinese Gods. "Chu Jong has decided the path for the rest of us. Monkey King and I are not so stupid to think we can play games with the elder Gods. He is blind, our Chu Jong. Blinded by his want of power."

"Blinded by boredom," Monkey King corrected and let out a screeching laugh. Loki found him by a tree. He looked less human than before. "I'll be back."

The creature scaled the tree and disappeared into the overgrowth.

"He does that. Sometimes I think he is still more monkey than man. Or God. He'll be back."

Loki nodded and took deeper breaths. He ached still. He would for a long time. He tried not to remember. . . .

"Why did Chu Jong want me? I can't believe he went through the trouble because Baldr wanted him to. In fact, I can't decide why he has Baldr at all."

"Baldr had been sniffing about our heavenly abode for many years. He'd been traveling with some Greeks for a long time, but they grew weary of his pretentiousness, so he searched for some other pantheon to plague. Chu Jong realized P'an Ku was awakening at about the same time. He fell in with Baldr and we have not quite found the reason. Baldr offers nothing."

"He most probably directed Chu Jong towards the Norse, though," Loki said. He leaned back. His head pounded. "He'd be the link to find Frigg. By taking her, Chu Jong might have thought to blind the Norse. But why me?"

"You are not one of them. You know this." Red leaned closer until his face was almost truly in focus. A serious face, with lines around his eyes and perhaps a little grey in his hair. "You are unpredictable, Loki. You are the unknown and everything the opposite of what Chu Jong sees as the future: order, symmetry, balance."

"I am chaos." He smiled. The movement of his face hurt, but he smiled anyway. "Which is why Odin came to me. He knew the Chinese Pantheon as a place of order. He said he wanted Chaos on his side."

"Wise, your Odin, but then he has a reputation for such."

"What do you intend to do with me?"

"Keep you away from Chu Jong until you are strong enough to deal with him and your Norse companions."

"Why aren't you marching in step with the rest of your pantheon?"

Red frowned and rested against a tree. "The others have mostly slept, you know. We have travelled in the ship, living in our own worlds for so long many had forgotten there was anything else. Chu Jong was one such. I am not certain what awoke him and brought him out of the cocoon. Monkey King and I . . . we become bored too easily with our own company. We kept awake, aware, moving. Quite often he and I directed the ship where we wanted."

"But not now."

"When Chu Jong awoke, he came with powers. They are more, I think, than he should have had. Something touched him, gave him strength and perhaps directed him to P'an Ku. I cannot guess why."

"Someone else directing him. Someone else awake?"

"There is one: the Queen of the West --"

"If so, we are in trouble," Loki said with growing worry. "She is more akin to the First Gods than to any of us."

"And we cannot know what she wants," Red Coat added. "You understand us very well."

"There are too many players." Loki shook his head. The movement hurt and the thoughts of someone else, more powerful, in the game, didn't help.

"And we have too little time. Rest while you can."

This seemed a very wise suggestion since he could barely move his arms and his head pounded to distraction. He tried to rest against the tree; not comfortable, but better than moving. The air felt too heavy and tasted of life and decay. He closed his eyes drawing small bits of power form the area around him. How long until Chu Jong realized he was gone?

"I admit I can't place Chu Jong," Loki said with a sigh.

"There are too many of you."

Red Coat gave a slight laugh. "True. He's a God of fire, the father of the dragon Kung Kung."

"Fire God and he's allied with a Norse? No, that's not right."

Red Coat didn't argue. "He was also charged with punishing those who broke the rules of Heaven. I suspect, perhaps, this is the heart of his obsession. He demands perfection and cannot find it even with the Gods, let alone elsewhere in creation."

Gods with obsessions were never good.

Loki felt somewhat better by the time Monkey King returned, giving a cry from the trees before he scrambled down beside Loki, moving as a monkey at first and then more human as he reached the ground.

"Here. This will help."

He tossed Loki a peach. Oh, not just *any* peach, of course. This one came fresh from the Garden of Immortal Peaches; power wrapped in guise of sun-warmed fruit. The Chinese Gods used the fruit to renew their immortality and Monkey King had a history of stealing them. Loki bowed his head in thanks -- a true thanks -- because this would do more than he could by stealing a little power from the air. Loki took a bite and felt the warmth spread through him, heady and sublime. Wounds began to heal and he felt better than he had in years.

"Chu Jong is mounting a group of soldiers to come this way," Monkey King reported. "He suspects we have taken this northerner. We need you strong so you can escape. I don't think we can hide you."

"I can hide myself. I am a shapeshifter, you know."

And he proved so by changing into a monkey -- a mostly normal one. The shape felt odd with the long arms and the different view. He didn't hold the shape for long and came back to himself with the peach still in hand. He took another bite.

"Oh, you are a tricky one, Loki!" Red laughed brightly. "Oh, yes, I can see why Chu Jong and Baldr worry so over you and what might happen. They should not have made you an enemy. Eat the peach."

"Remind me to give you an apple in return," he said. Apples were the Norse equivalent of peaches.

Monkey King hooted with laughter and gave a little dance. "Oh, I will, I will. And won't that stick in the craw of those silk-clad pompous fools?"

"The Norse won't be much happier," Loki replied. "A win all the way around, I'd say."

Red Coat laughed this time.

He was not fully healed when they heard Chu Jong coming. He couldn't have escaped yet anyway, so he changed into a monkey and climbed the tree. He scared off some birds and what might have been a snake. He had no love of serpents of any kind and luckily this one left on its own. He wanted revenge and any snake looked like an enemy right now.

Chu Jong marched into the area below, he and a hundred soldiers, spreading out around the trees. Surely he didn't think to surprise Loki, arriving with all this noise? Red Coat protested. Monkey King howled and leapt and seemed to both frighten and annoy Chu Jong.

Of course Chu Jong reacted badly. Monkey King represented nature and everything uncontrollable. Loki hadn't thought there could be worse than going to the primeval abyss and starting over, but now he had to consider other possibilities. If Chu Jong won, could he impose his vision of perfection on everything? Could this fool win the right from P'an Ku? The First Gods were capricious at best. They created things from nothing and placed order in the universe.

"I demand you return the northerner," Chu Jong shouted loud enough to be heard over Monkey King's hooting protest. His anger crackled about him, latent with destruction.

Leaves and branches whipped around Loki and he took tighter hold of the branch and waited. Chu Jong's mistake; with more power in the air it was less likely he could sense anything out of place.

"What northerner?" Red Coat demanded, giving a wave of his hand to silence Monkey King. And he did fall quiet in a sullen, gibbering way. They did the act well, the two of them.

"The one you released from the prison so you can make trouble --"

"What kind of fool are you, Chu Jong?" Red Coat demanded. "Have I not gone out of my way to avoid you and your plans? Why should I interfere with you now?"

"Who else would have done it?"

"What? You have no enemies? You have nothing but *loyal* allies, do you?"

Monkey King hooted with laughter this time, but he became more human again. "You are still a fool. You shouldn't have sent me away yesterday. I know more of P'an Ku than you ever will."

"And what will the knowledge help you?" Chu Jong demanded. "You sit here in your jungle doing nothing --"

"We get drunk. We laugh. We dance," Monkey King bounced around again. "We celebrate life, because if you win, everything joyful goes away. If you lose, everything goes away. We might as well enjoy ourselves."

Red Coat laughed agreement.

"Search!" Chu Jong ordered. The soldiers moved at his command; good little automatons, all of them. Red Coat and Monkey King sat on a log and drank good peach wine. They offered some to the guards. They even offered some to Chu Jong.

"You have him! You have him somewhere," Chu Jong shouted and looked up. Loki couldn't be certain if Chu Jong spotted him there in the shadows or not. Birds flew close by.

Other creatures shouted and yelled.

"Have you asked the Northerner Witch what happened to your prisoner?" Red Coat demanded, sounding annoyed. Loki could feel a new power building in the area. Monkey King let out another hoot, as though egging them on. "Have you asked your fine Baldr?"

"Have you asked the Queen of the West?" Monkey King suddenly asked.

The question won an instantaneous change in Chu Jong; a moment of uncertainty, which said a great deal. The two had guessed right about who might truly be behind this trouble, but the insight didn't make Loki feel any better.

Loki wanted Chu Jong to leave. Holding this form was not easy. He wanted out of the tree and, when he saw a snake twining his way, Loki very nearly decided he'd drop to the ground and face Chu Jong rather than sit here and share the tree with the serpent.

"Loki isn't here," Chu Jong declared. He took a step back, glanced around as though Loki might be standing right there beside him. "He isn't here, but if you had anything to do with his escape, I will know."

"Well, you better figure things out fast. You don't have a lot to time left," Red Coat replied and laughed.

Chu Jong spun and marched off, his men falling in around him.

Oh, but they didn't go far. Did Chu Jong really think he fooled anyone? He moved slightly out of sight and waited for some sign.

"More wine!" Monkey King shouted and howled. "We need more wine!"

Animals shouted in the trees. Birds swept by on all sides and, with a wave of his too-long arms, Monkey King created such chaos and noise it drove Chu Jong away, fleeing quickly from the jungle, his perfect soldiers barely keeping pace with him.

Loki slid down the tree trunk, stopped and sat before he changed. He leaned back, gasping, and accepted a beaker of the fine peach wine from Monkey King, sipping at the fresh flavor, the hint of life.

"See? This is a gentleman, you lout," Red said with a nod towards Loki. "You sip, not guzzle."

Monkey King gave a hoot of laughter again. Then he sat and daintily sipped his own wine. They all three laughed. Well, if the universe was going to end, maybe this wasn't such a bad way to go out.

CHAPTER TWENTY-SEVEN

D id they know anything, Red Coat and the damned Monkey King? He detested them both, sitting there in the filthy jungle, undisciplined and uncaring about the finer things Chu Jong represented.

They had asked questions he hadn't considered, though. Should he go to the Queen of the West? Should he ask her? Better, *far better,* to go to the Northern Witch and demand a reading. He needed to learn about Loki and Baldr and the truth of what was happening --

No.

Doubt was his enemy. Those two sowed the seeds of discord with their laughter and their smirking taunts. They sat in the jungle and hid because they had no control. Of course they did nothing at all. They never had.

He'd been looking in the wrong direction for answers. Baldr had set the bonds on Loki. He had expected Baldr to make them strong enough to hold his hated enemy, but he should have known better. This was his own failure because he trusted the work to such a lowly being.

He returned to his reality, leaving the jungle behind. The lowly staff bowed. He gave them no notice as he went to the north wing, where winter had set in again. He hurried past Frigg's suite and shivered to hear the laughter from within. What good did it do to hide the future from the Norse if she tampered with his own? He should have killed her and sent her to the abyss, but now was not the time to risk the repercussions from such an action. He should never have taken the woman into his household.

Into the *Emperor's* Household. He did not want to get ahead of himself. This was not truly his place. If the emperor had problems with the presence of the witch, surely he would have said to be rid of her. So would have the Queen of the West.

He went past her room without pause and crossed to Baldr's room. The pretentious bastard had put locks on his door. Chu Jong waved them away and went in without knocking.

Baldr leapt from his chair, reaching for this sword -- and pulled his hand away in time. Wariness and sanity warred in his face for a moment, but whatever he saw in Chu Jong's eyes stopped him from being too foolish.

"That was not wise, Chu Jong," Baldr said, an ominous sound as though he might have done his benefactor harm.

"Loki has gotten loose."

For a moment, Baldr didn't understand. Then he blanched. "Who let him go?"

"No one, you fool. Your magic failed. He got loose and, in this miasmic magic, we cannot track him." Seeing Baldr's panic, he knew the fool hadn't done this on purpose; a small recompense for having trusted him to do the work right. Chu Jong had been a fool and he didn't appreciate the feeling.

"Not *my* magic," Baldr replied, his eyes lighting with anger. The room grew colder, of course. They had no heat, even in anger, these damned northerners. "Someone released him. And he could be anywhere now. He could be *anyone*."

Baldr's hand went to the sword once more.

"I suggest you sleep with your sword if you think it will keep you safe," Chu Jong replied with a sneer. He left, content he had put the blame where it belonged.

The door slammed shut behind him, the locks doubled, as though they would stop him or Loki from entering.

He had forgotten Loki was a shapeshifter: a bad ability to overlook when dealing with such a creature. He tested everyone he passed for a hint of anything out of place. Damn them all for putting matters out of balance now, when time grew so short. He could feel the power of P'an Ku, growing stronger, the first breeze of a dangerous storm. They didn't have much time. No matter, no matter. The Northerners could not ruin his plans.

He hurried faster when he heard the witch laughing again.

CHAPTER TWENTY-EIGHT

T hey got drunk together, the three of them, and afterwards sobered (a good use for magic today) and left the jungle through a foggy wall in the *Imperial*. No door. Nothing so obvious. After a moment, Loki realized they had headed north, which Loki thought might be both figurative and symbolic. The jungle gave way to pine forest, the scent of home, trees shifting in shape around him.

"Where are we going?" he asked.

"We are getting you to the Norse," Red Coat replied. "You are safer with them."

"That doesn't say much, you know."

Monkey King, swinging through the trees above, hooted with agreement and somewhere near by a wolf howled. Loki knew the sound.

"Fenrir. He can be unruly. Keep back --"

The wolf bounded into the opening. Monkey King stayed in the trees. Red Coat took a step backwards, his hands raised, either in a show of peace or ready to use magic. Probably both.

"These two freed me from Baldr and Chu Jong," Loki explained in haste and moved to stand between the giant wolf and the Chinese God. He was never certain how much Fenrir understood in this form. "Safe, Fenrir."

The head tilted, the amber eyes blinking. Somewhere close by he could hear other voices and knew them to be northerners this time. He glanced at Red Coat.

Red Coat gave him an elegant little bow. "We'll go now and leave you to your own."

"Thank you. I'll do what I can, but --"

"You can repay us by making certain Chu Jong does not win."

"And if I don't . . . well, you two will have the peach wine for a while yet."

Red Coat laughed. Monkey King hooted in the tree and swung away, startling Fenrir. Red Coat backed away, watching the wolf with worry as Fenrir growled.

"No. Let him go."

Fenrir bowed his head. Red Coat turned his back to the wolf and walked away.

Loki moved to the nearest tree and leaned there. He could see a patch of the sky from here and what he had thought were clouds resolved into a mass of swirling power spewed out by the upcoming supernova. Colorful and pretty in its own way; but if someone didn't find a plan soon, they were not going to survive such beauty.

Torin arrived ahead of the others, the smile brightening his face. "I was right. Fenrir was coming after you! How the hell did you get out here?"

"With help from two of the Chinese who are no more enamored of Chu Jong and Baldr than we are." He pushed away from the tree and tried not to wince. "We need to do something. There isn't much more time."

"We know." Torin took his place by Loki's side and Loki felt stronger for his presence. "The others are . . . are more worried and subdued now."

Loki understood their feelings. He had begun to feel far less certain about what they could do. Every glance at the sky brought home the reminder that they were dealing with an Elder God and one who had been sequestered from the rise of humanity. They could have no common ground.

Fenrir trotted behind them, occasionally making a soft growl, though there didn't appear to be anything nearby to draw his attention. Tyr joined them as well; Loki must have heard Tyr and Torin talking. Hel came -- he had not expected her -- with the spirits tagging along, both she and her odd companions looking troubled. Could they not want the end? Wouldn't they want release? Not if all they had was oblivion to follow.

They weren't far from the Norse encampment near Bifrost. The magical path to *Asgard* still remained, bright and lovely, reaching upward to the stars. He wondered if he could go to the ship and rest for a while. Damn, he was tired.

He had not expected Odin to look so surprised and pleased when they appeared from the woods. Thor cast a less-than-angry glance his way, though he did not join his father in crossing to greet him.

"Fenrir said you were loose and he could scent you on the wind. I wasn't so sure," Odin admitted, but gave a bow to the wolf. Fenrir gave a little growl as he and Hel went aside again. They plainly wanted nothing to do with Odin.

Wiser than him.

"We don't have much time." Loki looked at the sky. Streamers of blues, greens and purples swirled over the top of the magic shield the Chinese had put around this world. He wondered how long the protection would hold. Not long enough. Either they came up with something to do soon or they lost.

"Come," Odin said and gave a little sign for silence. Odd. "Come and rest here for a bit."

Loki followed, curious because Odin wasn't one to care much about the comforts of others. They went to Bifrost and stepped upon the bridge, heading a few feet up from the ground.

"Sit as though you are resting here." Odin dropped to his

heels, facing him. The bridge painted them in pretty colors. "We think the Chinese can hear us if we are on the land, but not here, which is our own place."

"Ah. Devious." Loki sat, grateful to be off his feet.

"What few plans we made on land were intercepted. But Fenrir had come here to talk to Torin. When they left, we realized the Chinese didn't know why. So Tyr and Hel went to join them. You realized the point, Torin?"

"There is this thing called paper and writing," Torin said, pulling a piece of paper from his pocket. "Hel wrote me a note."

Odin gave an amused snort. "Good. What happened, Loki? We couldn't find you."

"Inside somewhere," he replied. He didn't want to recall the worst and repeat the tale to Odin. They were barely on speaking terms now and reminding him of the past, so lately relived, was not going to help. "Red Coat and Monkey God got me loose. They realized they don't want to be part of a regimented future."

"Wisdom in the ranks, then."

"Not much. They think the others never really woke and are now in Chu Jong's control," Loki added. "I don't know. There's talk of the Queen of the West and she might have her hand in this mess as well. How did they get Frigg?"

"There's a question I'll want answered one day." Odin glanced upwards and Loki followed his stare, surprised to see the Ravens in their old form. "I knew she had gone out. Shopping."

"Shopping," Loki repeated.

"She does sometimes," he replied with a shrug. "I think, really, she wants to be among humans. There is something in the connection she needs."

"Yes, I can understand," Loki admitted. He wondered if he should have said anything so honest about himself. Odin nodded though. He looked out to where Thor suddenly shouted. A group of Chinese came out, but they scurried inside once more as soon as the Norse set upon them.

"Cowards," Odin shouted, standing. Oh yes, he looked ready for the battle to begin again. Well, they might as well go down fighting. This might be the last chance at fleeting glory. If they didn't win, no one would be left to write myths about this one.

No. He wasn't ready to surrender yet.

"I don't understand what the Chinese -- what Chu Jong or the Queen of the West -- might expect in this," he admitted and hoped someone had an answer. "I don't know why they want to be here."

"This place," Odin said and looked over at the palace. "Bigger than when we first got here. Symbolic of their power?"

"Maybe. And power to spare here." Loki waved his fingers and cast a little fall of glittering lights before him. "The Chinese are big into signs, symbols and control."

"So this growing palace is their way of saying mine is bigger than yours?"

Loki snorted. "And is it a wonder they think the Norse are crude?"

"I have my reputation to maintain."

"Which has always been one of wisdom," Loki replied. He found himself looking at Odin, his head tilted. "And mine has been for treachery."

Odin winced. *Actually winced*, which surprised and unsettled Loki. He pushed the feeling away and looked at the clouds, which were not real clouds, and at the building that was not a real building.

"This is their place. They are trying to make us into what they want us to be. Chu Jong - he wants barbarians to put before P'an Ku."

"So he looks all the better."

"I would guess so, but he can't be that stupid, can he? Or maybe he is, but whoever is really pulling the strings . . . ."

"The Queen of the West."

"Let us assume so," Loki agreed. He glanced at the building. "But she isn't *here*, is she? She did not reside with the others, being one of the Elder Gods, who are more akin to the First Gods. More akin P'an Ku than Chu Jong."

"And she has more of an idea of what's going on." Odin glanced to the west.

"Maybe."

"We can't take the Chinese in a front-on attack and I think we're wasting our time besides. A few of us should see if there is anything to the West to help us. But we dare not let the Chinese know what we suspect. Who should go?"

"Me and mine," Loki replied. "Chu Jong fears I will stay and work with the Norse, so I should leave."

"Yes. Good idea," Odin agreed with a slight smile. He stood straighter and, with a well-placed foot, shoved Loki off the side of the bridge and onto the ground.

Surprise and anger spread through him as he surged to his feet. Then he almost laughed at the sight of shocked and dismayed Norse who had been watching the drama. Loki spun and headed for the woods to get away as soon as fast as he could, pulling in chaos around him to help confuse Chu Jong. He didn't look to see who followed, but he could hear Torin -- knew the sound of him running to catch up. Four feet followed, so he knew Fenrir came along as well. He suspected Hel, but he didn't turn to see.

"Koil?" Torin asked.

He lifted his chin to the woods. Distance, he hoped, would make a difference. "I need to get away from them. The Norse and the damned Chinese."

Torin might have caught the implications since he was a smart kid. At any rate, he kept silent as they moved on, Fenrir guarding their backs. Hel moved closer, her ghostly companions drifting around her and brushing against Loki sometimes; cold things leaving a hint off winter ice on his skin.

Loki let his rage linger. Not really difficult, because so many things had happened since this farce began. He released a little magic in each step, mostly useless tendrils, but some testing for the feel the Chinese. He hoped he gave them a headache with each little jab. He and his companions went on into the trees and the touch of the Chinese grew fainter as they moved away from the palace.

He stopped finally and rested once more with a tree to keep him to his feet. Maybe he needed to grow a few trees on the station. He found he enjoyed the feel of something solid and alive at his back.

"Since the Chinese can listen to what we are doing by the Palace, we had to get clear of the area," Loki explained finally. He took a deeper breath, not really up to this kind of hike. He pushed away from the tree and started on again. No time to rest. "We think there is another player. Someone with more power and cunning than Chu Jong. Oh, yes, the Queen of the West is far more dangerous."

Fenrir moved to walk beside him and slowly changed to human form. He didn't look particularly comfortable. However, he gave a nod. "Tell us about her. What should we expect?"

So, Loki's interest in the other pantheons paid off. They walked through the woods and he quickly repeated all he could of the stories he knew. The Queen of the West, Hsi Wang-mu held court on her mountain and dispensed prosperity and longevity. She was especially associated with women. The facts were not, he thought, very helpful, but at least the others knew what they were dealing with this time.

He had not expected the Queen of the West to come to them. She stepped out of somewhere else and into the woods barely two yards away, a growling white tiger at her side. Fenrir changed in a heartbeat, matching growl with growl.

Not the kind of battle Loki wanted to see. He reached over and tapped Fenrir on the shoulder, feeling the muscles tense, the wolf unwilling to back down. He tapped a second time while the tiger's ears went flat and he crouched, ready to leap.

Fenrir stepped back, a growl low in his throat, but willing to obey. The Queen of the West snapped her fingers and the tiger obeyed as well.

"So, better trained than Fenrir," Loki said.

She gave him a cold smile. Loki would have thought her old and plain, but light shown around her in a nimbus beauty and he admitted she had an icy charm all her own, something the Norse could appreciate. The smile, though, promised nothing good and he'd already had enough of unpleasant Chinese Gods of late.

"You would do well to not mettle in matters you don't understand. You might not survive," she warned, her voice cool as the breeze blowing past them.

None of them were much bothered by the show, though. In fact, Loki welcomed it, this cold that reminded him of the north and home long ago. This was, perhaps, a Goddess he might understand.

"And if we step away, will we survive?" Loki asked.

"No."

"Then we really don't have anything to lose, do we?" he asked.

Her eyes narrowed. Was she too used to the Chinese who bowed and walked away, knowing she ruled their lives? She was not *his* Goddess and though he respected the abilities of others, he was not going to do as she expected.

"Fenrir, can you take the tiger?" he asked.

Fenrir growled, a low sound, eager to try; the cat answered, ears going flat again. No normal tiger, of course. The cat understood quite as easily as Fenrir did.

"And what would this prove?" The Queen of the West demanded, ice in her voice this time, the cold brushing against the trees and the leaves tinkling like glass bells.

"Not much -- but if Fenrir takes him, this upsets the balance, right? Isn't the balance what this is all about?" What did she want, he wondered? What could she win from this very odd scenario? "This is all about balance, power . . . and you taking over when Chu Jong fails."

He had taken a guess and hit something at least close to the truth. The tiger looked startled, though Loki saw nothing more than a blink of her eyes.

"You do not understand," she replied, her head shaking and white hair lifting and falling as though gravity meant nothing to it, a gentle flow of movement, without breeze, without any connection to the world. She had cut herself off too long ago.

She was the one who couldn't understand them. She couldn't begin to explain in terms that related to others.

"You've lost your connection. You're losing control. You're losing yourself."

Her head lifted, her eyes blazing. When her hand lifted, his heart pounded as he saw his own destruction in her face.

But the hand lowered. Control returned to her face. Her hair changed, darker now, elaborately coifed in a style Loki remembered from a very old porcelain, as though she called back old memories and old controls. "Oh, if only *you* had been mine, rather than that fool Chu Jong. If we had worked together -- too late now, young fool. Too late. I gave Chu Jong ambition to come here, where I could . . . be with P'an Ku, who is akin to me. Chu Jong fed the little ambition to create something for himself and now he moves more and more on his own. I put this trouble in motion, nudging P'an Ku, wanting to connect with something I had known so very long ago. None of us will survive."

She spun with a sparking of ice crystals, took a step . . . and disappeared.

"Well, that was certainly enlightening and oh-so-uplifting," Torin said in the sudden silence. "Why the hell did she come out here?"

Loki stared where she had gone, everything sorting out in his mind. He gave a belated bow to her because she had done them a kindness. "She came to see if we understood and to save us a long journey in time and magic we don't have to waste."

Torin stared, his face paling slightly now. "So, she can't admit it, but she hopes we can do something."

"Yes. Because otherwise she could have destroyed us where we stand. She may be weaker than she has been in the past, but she isn't weak in any sense we understand. She cannot connect, but she can destroy."

"So what do we do?" Hel asked.

Fenrir changed to human, though he continued to pace. "I wanted to take the tiger," he finally admitted, a bit of a growl in his voice.

"Ah. Sorry," Loki replied and tried not to laugh. "Maybe you'll still have a chance. Or you could take Chu Jong."

"Could I?" he asked and his amber eyes brightened at the thought.

"Carefully," Loki said and put a hand on his shoulder. They had long since stopped being father and son, but they had ties. "All three of you, be very careful . . . but go for Chu Jong if you can. We need him out of the picture. She no longer controls her puppet, which makes the fool very dangerous. I think if we can disorganize the Chinese, we can win against them."

"And what does winning against the Chinese get us?" Torin asked. "They are not, really, the problem are they? There is still P'an Ku."

"True," Loki agreed, glancing around the woods. They

dared not stay here long. "But they are going to stop us from doing anything about the real problem even if we happen to stumble across a plan somewhere."

The other three nodded agreement. He couldn't be certain what they thought or believed, though. It was enough, he guessed, for them to trust him. As he walked away, they fell in around him.

"Are we going back to the camp?" Torin asked.

"No. I think if we stay clear, we can have a better chance of doing something unexpected," Loki said. "But we need to be closer. And out of the woods where I can see the sky better."

"How long do you think the magic shell the Chinese put around this world will hold?" Torin asked.

"Not long enough. Get to Bifrost as fast as you can if the magic starts to crack. That's our best hope for safety and I really can't say the bridge will hold."

He was taking account of everything now, but found nothing good. Lack of time, lack of allies, lack of a plan. He didn't want to despair, but he suddenly had the feeling he might not walk away from this one. He wouldn't return to Sigyn and, if this went to P'an Ku, she wouldn't survive either. Nothing would . . . and all because an ancient Goddess had reached for something she should never have tried to waken. Lonely. Lost among the stars.

Loki refused to despair. Time to act as though they would win and grab hold of any symbolism they could. They had precious little else going for them.

CHAPTER TWENTY-NINE

Chu Jong felt something odd in the air . . . a slight breeze from a distant winter. The Queen of the West whispered on the breeze, but he didn't hear her clearly this time. He thought she might be angry with him. If so. . . .

If so, she could come here and tell him.

He kept his attention on the Norse. They were gathered in their groups, grunting and arguing as though they were nothing more than animals. He imagined them so, all in their native costumes -- the skins of wild animals -- stomping through the snow on their way to devour some fresh kill. Animals. *Barbarians.* And stupid ones. They didn't know he could hear them prepare their attacks. They kept throwing themselves against the palace and the Chinese fought them aside with no trouble. They were not very inventive.

This was his place. His world. His decisions would make the future.

His heart soared at the thought. Him, forever in charge of everything. The ultimate power, the ultimate riches. He would have what he wanted and deny existence itself to those whom he detested.

He need never deal with fools again.

Yes, fools. He glared as Monkey King and Red Coat sauntered out of the forest and into the camp. They laughed and insulted the guards at the edges of the building where they waited for the barbarians to attack again. With a flick of his wrist he could have sent the guards against the two . . . but this would not be wise, here in the open where others could see. He didn't hold enough power to simply destroy them himself *yet* and the other Gods were starting to get restless. He dared not do something which might upset the precarious balance.

Chu Jong couldn't imagine why the two came here, except to annoy him. They didn't disappoint him, either. They both gave low, mocking bows while Monkey King howled with animal laughter and drew stares from everyone. The wise ones pretended not to see, but he was aware of the Norse watching as well, seeing him mocked by these two.

"What do you want?" Chu Jong demanded.

"Oh, many, many things," Red Coat replied. "But not so much as what you want, I think."

He scowled, which did no good with these two who were not wise enough to know they shouldn't annoy him. "Go. Leave. You are not here to help."

"Help you end the universe?" Monkey King asked. Far too serious, which drew attention of a different sort. Startled looks. Worried looks. Damn this creature to all the hells mankind had ever created!

"You do not know what I'm doing," he snarled, his voice lowering, stilling his hands before they formed into fists, while the cold wind whispered around him again. He ignored her call once more, but the other two must have noticed. They frowned all the more.

"No, *you* don't know what you're doing," Red Coat replied. Too serious there as well and others, both guards and Gods, stared. What did these fools want? To take some of his glory? "And the others are too used to not looking."

"Leave. Leave before I am tempted --"

"Too fight us?" Red Coat smirked. "To dirty your pretty

silken robes? Not you, oh great Chu Jong."

"When I win --"

"Ha!" Monkey King laughed, a loud animal hoot. "Ha! You will never rule us. You are a fool and a braggart. A thief of others' dreams, a demon in the night --"

He didn't know why the words angered him so. He shouted and lifted his hands to cast. He called upon the very powers of the heavens and the magic came to him: oh yes, the power came to him in a rush of glory and power, melting into his body and burning through his soul. His power. His place! He yelled with the power and --

They were gone.

"Cowards!" he screamed and sent the power flying. Trees fell before him. He knew they had gone hiding into their woods. "Cowards, face me and my wrath! Face your doom!"

Everyone ran before his glory. He laughed and the ground trembled at the sound. He waved his hands and the wind moved, knocking over everything. The Norse retreated to their damned rainbow. He would destroy them even there --

He tired suddenly, an exhaustion so overwhelming it frightened him. He knew he dared not show the weakness. He forced his head up, glaring at those few who were hidden nearby. "Fools! All of you fools!" He headed into the building, walking steadily through the doors and on towards his rooms, forcing himself not to slow where the servants might see -- on and on --

Behind the safety of his pure white door he fell to his knees. His heart pounded and everything roared in his ears. How dare they force him into a show of power and put everything he planned in danger!

Chu Jong knelt there for a long time, accepting the peace of the perfect cherry orchard that filled the space before him. Calm did not come, but plans did. He would watch the others wither in pain as he took all of them apart, piece by piece and sucked the power from their very bones. The image pleased him. He calmed again.

CHAPTER THIRTY

"Well done," Odin said, surprising Loki. The small shield Odin made protected Loki and his group from detection. Even Red Coat and Monkey King had joined them while Chu Jong raged. The distraction had gone very well and the fact everyone ran in haste helped them get to the safety of the bridge. Now they could discuss whatever they pleased.

Too bad they still had no plan.

Monkey King appeared very interested in the bridge, tapping the surface and sniffing the magic. Red Coat was far more interested in the sky. Loki felt his heart catch at the sight of swirling eddies spreading wider as he watched. They'd run out of time, he feared.

Well, he was never very good at waiting anyway.

"P'an Ku isn't going to wait for us to devise a plan." Loki turned to the others. Monkey King, sitting low in the midst of the Norse so he went unnoticed, gave a little hoot of laughing agreement, which reminded Loki of something else.

"You have a tie to P'an Ku, Monkey King," Loki said, drawing the odd God's attention. "You were born of a rock left over from his time, right? From his shell?"

"Oh, smarter than our fine and ambitious Chu Jong," Monkey King replied and seemed to mean those words. "He did not consider such a thing and, when I reminded him, the fool asked nothing of me. Not that I would have helped him."

"What can you tell us? What will help?"

He could see Monkey King's face, which suddenly appeared so human he thought even Red Coat looked a little startled. "I can tell you there was a moment, between when the shell cracked and before I came fully into the world, when I felt . . . lost. When I was neither myself nor something new; if the shell had fallen in on me, I would not have come out for a good long time."

"Well." Odin looked at the sky. "That's a damned large shell to shove back into place."

"It's going to take a hellish lot of power. Maybe more than we can manage," Tyr added. He looked towards the building. "Can we get help from the Chinese?"

"Not so long as Chu Jong is in charge of them," Red Coat replied with the answer Loki had expected. "He wants to be the Great One, in charge of the universe. He thinks he can win this from P'an Ku by showing the Chinese as perfect and the Norse as chaotic. I'm uncertain if he even sees the third choice, where P'an Ku destroys everything. None can talk to him. Sometimes if you say we need to do one thing, he will, against all logic, do something else."

Monkey King nodded agreement and slouched, more monkey than human once more. Loki found the constant shapeshifting a distraction.

"And how do we take out Chu Jong?" Odin asked. "Apparently a straight-up battle isn't going to work, is it? We've been trying and getting nowhere."

"Not likely," Red Coat agreed. He gave a nod towards the building. "That is the seat of his power, you know. His suite is the nexus of what he is and there he has created a perfect world within his little corner of the universe. If the perfection is marred, he is weakened. However, this won't be easy, either. He has safeguards and he fears everyone stealing his thunder."

"But we can do it," Loki said. "We must."

"We need to move now." Odin once again glanced to the sky, his face showing worry. "How do we get into the building?"

"We take Loki in," Red Coat said. "Loki alone, because his chaos is the best weapon against Chu Jong's perfection and taking more of you would be noticeable. Chu Jong can't know we're coming or else he will lock the door against Monkey King and me. This is not the obvious door, you understand. Not the one through which he comes out to do battle, which is a symbolic door linked to his power. The other, lesser door is never obvious until opened. He might have locked us out anyway, since we irritated him, but I do not think so. His thoughts are not directed towards us now. He grows in power and he doesn't quite know how to handle what he covets. I think we can sneak in, as long as he is busy elsewhere."

Red Coat looked to Odin.

"I'll get the others ready for an attack," Odin said. He glanced to the sky and away again, his mouth set and his face holding a hint of battle lust. Loki would have preferred calculation. "The others won't need to know more. We'll throw enough magic at the building to cover what is going on."

"Blind him with power," Monkey King agreed with a nod.

So, finally, they had a plan. Of sorts. Loki looked around at the others, none of them any more hopeful than him. A glance at the sky showed they had no time to plan anything better.

CHAPTER THIRTY-ONE

Amused, P'an Ku thought, testing out a word he had not known before. Yes, amused to listen to thoughts, odd and garbled. Magic traced its way nearby, some pieces cold and hard but with a rare beauty. . . .

Two groups stood close by, poised for battle. Fascinating little ants, these creatures. Build their empires, move their pieces, and those with powers and magic not so different from the others.

Not what he had created before he slept, though.

Not what he had expected.

Not what he wanted.

And yet . . . and yet. . . .

Fascinating to look out at them for a while longer. He had no reason to rush. Time meant nothing to him.

CHAPTER THIRTY-TWO

Frigg threw the runes, knowing this would be the last time before everything moved along whatever path resolved out of this chaos. She could see the abyss in her mind's eye, taking almost all her sight and leaving her blind to much of the real world. Even so, she couldn't be certain it would be the future.

Something had changed and she frowned at the runes, trying to make sense of this new twist. She hadn't expected a change this time, but she found an odd line running through the runes; a trail of power showed both treachery and hope.

She ran her fingers over the runes and gathered them up. Finally time to go. She'd stayed too long with the Chinese. She wanted away from Chu Jong and his mindless followers.

Mindless. Why had such a thought never occurred to her before?

Someone moved them. Not Chu Jong, though he had some influence. She pulled her shawl tighter around her, feeling the cold come close again. And Frigg knew, now, where she had to go. Not to Chu Jong, who wasn't as powerful as he had been just hours before. Everything fluctuated.

Baldr came to her door, white-faced with fear and worry. She glared at him and he backed away.

"Do not bother me," she ordered, her voice as cold as any northern winter. "Don't come near me or I might be tempted to something you would regret."

"How can you say such a thing to me? We are both trapped here --"

"Shall I read for you, Baldr?" she asked and held the runes out in her hand, the stones glittering balefully with power. "Are you ready for your fate?"

He backed away, his tongue brushing over his lips. "No. I do not want to hear such tricks from you. You might say anything and make me believe."

"You would not believe the truth; you never have. But you are not so much a fool to think you have any friends here, right?"

"We should stand together. We should --"

"Be gone, Baldr," she ordered and her voice held ice and northern winds, the cold rage of a time long past, but still part of her soul. "Go to your oh-so-civilized friends and speak to them of the future. But do so quickly. None of us have much time left."

"They'll gain control. They'll win. We will not die here and return to the beginning. Not again."

"Why not? What will stop us?"

"The Chinese can --"

She waved those words away with a flick of her hand. He leapt back, obviously expecting magic. And just in spite, she sent some out; pretty lights, nothing more. Frigg's nature prevented her from doing battle and fighting because she could see the person's fate was already settled. Baldr had come to this place on his own. He'd made this journey through one short death and returned to repeat the same mistakes again. Maybe everything returning to the beginning would save them from having to relive this drama another time. Starting over gave a chance for change and maybe they would all be different the next time.

Or they might not be anything ever again. She wondered if

she would not prefer the absolute end to another round of this madness.

Baldr backed all the way out of her room. She went after him and he fled down the hall. She snarled a curse at his back, though nothing serious. The myth would change. He was no longer the best of them all. Time to let the legend go and bring something new into a world where the Gods were not what they had been.

Time to change things. She started walking the other direction, heading to the west.

CHAPTER THIRTY-THREE

L oki stood on the wide path of Bifrost, other Norse close by and Red Coat and Monkey King beside him. Both their Chinese allies looked more serene than he expected, given the situation. No one, after all, had spoken about actually winning.

"So, you think this will work?" Loki dared ask.

Red Coat laughed this time. "I think it hardly matters if this plan doesn't work, my friend. So I will say thank you now."

"Why?"

"For giving us this chance to do something unusual," he replied and his companion nodded with enthusiastic agreement. "We have a chance to step out of our own limited myths and into a different world. Perhaps we should thank Baldr as well, though I doubt very much that he would appreciate the sentiment."

"Baldr has much to answer for." Loki looked ahead at where Odin and Thor spoke, preparing to leave the bridge and rush to the building. Not long now. And, really, he was glad. Time to be done with this round of madness.

"He is trapped, you know. He has no choice," Red Coat said.

Loki shook his head. "No. None of us are trapped or forced to turn against our own kind. If so, I should have been the worst enemy of this group, right? I should have worked to ruin them. But I didn't."

"You wanted to, though."

"Yes. For centuries I let the anger direct me. But I've changed. Baldr could have as well, if he'd wanted to."

They didn't argue. This might have been an interesting philosophical discussion at another time. But right now -- no. Odin gave the nod. Finally. Time to move.

Loki felt a wave of amazement at how well the Norse rushed forward as a group, aimed towards a common goal. He went with them, feeling the heat of the battle, thinking he could understand the berserkers and their willingness to let go, though he never wanted to lose himself and kill without thought or mercy.

They were within yards of the building before Chu Jong finally realized his troops were not holding them back this time. Loki saw more of the Chinese warriors forming into lines at the door and suspected Chu Jong might be creating from nothing at all, which would explain why so many of them simply disappeared. The Norse shouldn't have any trouble pushing those insubstantial puppets aside. They simply needed to get inside.

Closer. Red Coat and Monkey King remained side by side, well-hidden behind the taller Norse. Odin sent waves of magic against the enemy and the building, as though he meant to force his way in, masking the real plan.

Chu Jong arrived with his head high as he directed his troops to line up and prepare to throw themselves against the enemy. Everything on the Chinese side was in the proper place, which was whatever Chu Jong decided. No need for his warriors to think. No need to decide. Simply move and do as he directed.

And into this carefully arranged world, the Norse were about to throw chaos.

Loki had been holding back for so long he had nearly lost

touch with the core of his power and the essence of what he truly represented. As he called upon the tendril that always rested within his heart, he felt the power grow and had to keep control or he might cause trouble for his own people. Chaos didn't favor one side over the other. However, the chaos would mostly affect those who counted on control and who thought perfect rank and action would win the day.

He let the power loose, a little in one direction, more in another -- no one would notice amidst all the other magic here until the accumulation played against them.

Loki smiled. Chu Jong had made two big mistakes, as far as Loki could tell. He had ignored Monkey King because the God was not sedate enough for him and could not be controlled, and he had chosen to make Loki an enemy rather than an ally -- because, he realized, Chu Jong had no allies. He had people who obeyed him and he had the Queen of the West who directed him until he severed his tie with her because he could not order her.

Fool. Loki wondered how the man got this far into power. The realization of how little help Chu Jong could call upon gave him hope as they moved closer. In another few steps they would clash and he feared for a moment Fenrir had failed --

No. He heard the growl, low and ominous like distant thunder. Chu Jong looked around in surprise.

Fenrir came in a streak of grey and black, moving so quickly Loki barely marked his passage until the wolf leapt at Chu Jong's throat. The God barely moved aside in time to save his life, but the wolf dug teeth deep into Chu Jong's shoulder. He shrieked with pain and anger. Something huge and darkly luminous came from Chu Jong's shadow, an evil launched from the God's own soul. Fenrir had the wisdom to leap out of the way. The thing grew longer, black arms reaching and twining around Fenrir, who let out a yelp of protest and pain.

Torin rushed to help Fenrir while the others exploded into

battle around them. Shouts and screams arose from the Norse while the Chinese moved on in their mindless silence, pitting themselves against the barbarians. As long as Chu Jong kept busy –

A cold, dead wind passed overhead and Hel swarmed in, her ghostly followers sweeping around Chu Jong who gave another startled cry. The shadow creature lost the grip on Fenrir and the soldiers seemed to lose direction.

Odin hadn't missed the moment. He turned his attention from the attack of the mindless soldiers and focused on Chu Jong. With a shout of his own, Loki leapt forward and threw himself into the fray.

And that was when they learned Chu Jong did have important allies who were not mindless drones. The door to the building burst open and Loki, caught far too much in the forefront with Torin, Fenrir and Hel, had the dubious pleasure of seeing Tialong burst forth in all his dragon glory, followed by a line of Chinese Gods with the Emperor himself in the lead.

Symbolically, the Chinese had played the trump card. Dragons and Emperors were metaphorically stronger than anything the Norse could bring to the battle. Loki worried --

To hell with that. He'd never played fair before.

He reached into his jacket, pulled out a laser pistol, and shot the Emperor.

Being a near mortal -- closer to humans than to the Gods -- made him vulnerable. The Chinese, revering their Emperor, meant they would not have expected him to be a target, since he was little more than a standard bearer. However, Loki knew the power of such positions. His shot cut through the fancy lacquered armor and straight through the Emperor's heart. The figure remained still for a moment before he toppled forward. For a brief heartbeat of time, everything froze while symbols reordered and powers were lost and gained.

The dragon reacted before anyone else. The scream of rage

might have deafened a lesser being as the creature surged forward, unerringly aimed at Loki.

"Damn!" He scrambled backwards, bringing the pistol around again. He didn't think the tech weapon would work so well on the dragon, so he grabbed at some chaotic power and sent in a flash light, a sparkling of green and blue power twisting through the air. The creature backed away a step, slowing for a precious moment. Loki used the distraction to aim the laser . . . and shot Chu Jong.

Not a clean kill like the emperor. The God had wrapped himself in magic, but the laser cut through the power. Not as good as cutting through the armor but his shot found flesh and Chu Jong went to his knees.

Loki left him for the others. He had a dragon to deal with now. A very mad dragon who had seen the emperor, whom he had served for eternity, killed before his eyes. This might not have been Loki's wisest move, especially since he didn't have a lot of help right now. Fenrir, Hel and Torin were busy keeping Chu Jong busy and even if he trusted Odin and Thor, he wasn't certain they could get free to help him.

The Valkyrie swept in, attacking the dragon, much to Loki and the creature's surprise. They held the dragon's attention, but they were no match for the creature. Loki wasn't certain he would be either, but he charged forward, ducking below claws and rolling aside when the huge gapping mouth snapped at him. A claw caught his side, ripping clothing and skin. He yelled and swept his hand up, laser fire and magic power aiming at the one vulnerable spot he could find -- the eyes. He managed to hit the left one.

A dragon enraged and now in uncontrollable pain turned out not to be any better. Loki scrambled out of the way, doing his best to stay to the left side where the dragon couldn't clearly see him. Could he blind the right eye? Killing the dragon would be better, but Tialong was powerful and they were running out of time.

Killing the emperor had at least demoralized the soldiers the Chinese Gods kept throwing at them. The Norse were still having a little trouble with their battle because of the seemingly endless supply of the soldiers rushing out of the building.

Monkey God and Red Coat? He couldn't see either of them.

The dragon swept out with his tail and hit Loki hard enough to lift him. He would have landed amid all those Chinese Gods if he hadn't shape-changed in midflight and taken the form of an eagle.

Oh, and didn't that annoy them? He thought about doing something rather crass . . . but his attention shifted to the overall battle and he could see how they were about to have some serious trouble. Chinese Gods led these drones in person and the group slipped through the edge of the woods off to the right of the building. He gave a cry of alert and flew towards the trouble. One of the Ravens pointed and Odin had the wisdom to mark his flight. Barely in time, too, as the Chinese swarmed out of the woods, yelling their battle cry.

From above the battle, Loki saw a troubling difference between the free men of the Norse and the drones of the Chinese. The Imperial Army moved at a whim from Chu Jong and probably some of the others. The Norse needed orders and moved more slowly to redirect, which almost led a disaster in those few crucial seconds of surprise.

Loki couldn't take on either horde of soldiers and do any good, so he focused on the Gods. With a cry of defiance, he swept into the midst of them, pecking and clawing, and came away with nothing more than some feathers singed.

The ploy wouldn't work again, but for a moment he had broken their hold on the soldiers as the Norse swept in among them, giving their own shout of battle. Odin, seeing the Chinese Gods unsettled, leapt towards Chu Jong again. Thor, with the mighty Mjuolnir, headed straight for the mass of Gods.

He couldn't find any sign of Tialong and suspected the dragon had gone with the emperor, to guard him still. That might give them a better chance. Unless the dragon only went into the building . . . but he had no sense of it anywhere.

Another sweep through the sky showed the Valkyrie collecting the dead from the field since a number of the Norse warriors had fallen already. If this played out too long, the Chinese would win through attrition.

He saw Skuld hit with a bolt of power and he wasn't alone in crying out in shock and dismay as she fell, though she disappeared in a flash of light before she hit the ground. Gone. They would be a long time before she returned.

Several Valkyrie screamed in rage and swept out of the skies towards a knot of Chinese Gods. Another Valkyrie fell and disappeared but, when the women pulled back, none of the Chinese Gods had survived. The battle had been quick and decisive.

Loki found Tyr in trouble. Two of the Chinese Gods had broken away from the others and were dragging Tyr towards the building. Did they know he was the God of War? Loki didn't think much about Tyr's position in the pantheon. Did they think depriving the Norse of their link to war would make them less fierce?

Loki dropped straight at them, but an eagle wasn't going to win against these two. He changed before he hit the ground, landing with as much grace as he could manage. He was weakened in magic after his shapeshifting display, but he could kick. The one trying to hold Tyr by the arm did a little flying of his own. Tyr threw the other one off and gave a bright smile to Loki and a nod of thanks.

Damn, he'd missed the camaraderie. Loki hadn't realized how much until then. He stood side-by-side with Tyr and fought off any who tried to take them. Not an easy battle. Tyr was already bloodied and the enemy was not backing off.

Loki took a bad cut through the side from someone behind. He twisted as he went to his knees, gasping.

Baldr.

Ragged, his hair snarled, his clothing dirty; the sight surprised Loki. He hadn't looked this bad at their last meeting. Baldr snarled, animal-like and leapt forward, meaning to kill Tyr this time, the sword already red with Loki's blood. Loki grabbed at him, startling the man and winning Tyr a moment to see the situation.

Unfortunately, Thor had seen as well.

Thor, enraged, charged straight for Baldr, the proverbial bull in a china shop. Loki struggled to his feet, uncertain if he wanted to stop Thor, who didn't appear aware of the half-dozen Chinese Gods heading for them. Loki stepped forward, but Thor snarled and swept him aside with a growl and Loki, winded and wounded, landed at the feet of the two Gods he had fought away from Tyr.

Oh damn.

He tried to roll away, but they caught him and Tyr who had come to help.

Loki thought Odin might have gotten Thor in hand because he saw Baldr running towards the building. The Chinese quickly dragged Loki to the building. H

Before they dragged him inside, he saw the sky . . . and what might be two gigantic red eyes staring through a ragged crack at them.

He hoped P'an Ku enjoyed the show.

Chapter Thirty-Four

C hu Jong nearly screamed his frustration as power grew within him, ready to explode out and destroy --

But no. *No.* He must hold on and pull back. He must take control and not let himself become one with the chaotic battle. If he wanted to control the universe, he could not lose himself to the base emotions the Norse brought with them.

He had downed the damned wolf and his allies, though he wasn't certain if any of them were dead. Evil, unnatural creatures! They should never have been brought to a battle of this importance. He had fought Odin himself, power against power -- no base flashing of swords and spilt blood for them. No win there, but no loss either, and Odin had been the one to retreat. The Norse army slipped away at last, wounded and weak. He wanted to kill them, but he hadn't the time to waste on the defeated.

Then he saw something which ensured he would win. The Chinese had captured both Loki and another of the powerful Norse.

He had what he wanted. With Loki in hand, the others had no real weapon against him. He thought they might realize their loss. Some had started to back away in haste. Odin and Thor made their stands and the women of the skies swept at them, trying to reach their lost brethren, but they were too late. Too late! The others dragged the two into the building.

Chu Jong laughed and the world shook around him. He raised his fist into the sky --

He could see P'an Ku there. P'an Ku *watching*. Now was not the time to mimic the barbarians. He gave a bow to the greater God and retreated to his building. He did not run, though his heart pounded with fear. He must not show these emotions before the ancient God. He must show he is worthy.

They had dragged the captives inside, through the lesser door, where servants and prisoners entered into the glorious Imperial Palace. Chu Jong walked sedately towards the larger door, his head high, his power assured. P'an Ku would judge him worthy.

The door would not open for him.

CHAPTER THIRTY-FIVE

The Chinese Gods had dragged Loki through the small door and into the building. Tyr tried to fight, but Loki didn't. Wasn't this where he wanted to go? And they had not bound him in any way. Their mistake to discount him and what he could do. So he waited, waited --

And they were inside.

Loki acted so quickly he even took Tyr by surprise. He pulled free of one of the Chinese and shouted as he shot power out in all directions; hard to control something so close to the edge of chaos, but he didn't want to take Tyr down with the others so he dared not simply let go. Neither did he want to hit Red Coat or Monkey King who had joined in a battle by the ornate red door.

Loki grabbed Tyr by the arm and rushed through the soldiers, killing four or five, who disappeared from the scene in a quick succession of flashes.

"Well," Monkey King said. "That's one way to get inside."

"Ah, but trouble!" Red Coat warned with a frantic shake of his head. He had a hand on the door. "Chu Jong is coming. If he comes in --"

"Back!" Loki shouted, a hand to his bleeding side as he stumbled forward.

The others leapt away and Loki sent every bit of chaotic power he could manage against the door, there in the heart of the enemy's stronghold. Much of the power bounced off, but he could see the door had been singed, the sockets melted. This door was not going to open.

He had just symbolically deprived Chu Jong of the door to his power. He could come in through the common door, but the act would cost him. Loki hoped this would be enough because he was going to his knees and he had the feeling maybe he wouldn't get back up --

They were carrying him. Undignified for a God. He squirmed and cursed and, through half-closed eyes, he saw the curse become an unruly flash of purple, bouncing across the walls.

"Stop," Tyr warned. "We have enough problems!"

"Down," he said. "Feet on floor. Connection."

Tyr must have understood. They lowered him so his feet touched the floor. Tyr had done a quick job of stopping his side from bleeding, though everything hurt like hell again. His vision darkened and spots appeared, but he refused to fall. He could hear battle and tried to see --

"Don't. We haven't time to waste. We need to get to Chu Jong's suite."

Loki remembered the plan. He looked ahead where Monkey King led the way, which probably meant Red Coat fought the battle pressing in from behind. Tyr kept him to his feet as they moved and Monkey King danced ahead, shape-changing so quickly that sometimes he walked as a human and other times he gamboled ahead on his knuckles and back again. Their guide had to slow when Loki couldn't keep up. Unfortunately, the battle behind them pushed faster now, closing in on them. Not much time.

The halls changed with a sense of veneration and stillness with each step. They should not rush here. This was a place to contemplate, to whisper words and find calm, pattern, symmetry with life --

"Oh hell." He shook his head and looked at Tyr and Monkey King. They had no trouble moving. "This is not good."

"Loki?" Tyr asked. He sounded distant, although he held onto Loki's arm.

"Opposites. And his place. His way overcoming. . . ." But Loki lost what he meant to say. He stared at the pattern of the floor tiles, perfection where they placed their feet.

Tyr grabbed hold of his chin, pulling his head up and staring into Loki's face. "Oh, no, you aren't getting out of the trouble this easy. You got us in here and you are going to finish the job this time."

"What do you mean, *this time*?" Loki demanded. He pulled away, glaring --

And Tyr grinned. "Well, that finally got your attention. We're here."

He frowned, then laughed, realizing Tyr had purposely annoyed him to bring him back. He hoped it didn't have to happen again, because being annoyed was not his best reaction.

Monkey King waited in front of a door; white and pristine, with no handle or any other sign of a way inside. Loki felt as though a layer of perfection had become real and stood guardian before him. It radiated smugness as though Loki was the most unworthy of all beings and would never dare cross such a threshold. The door repelled him.

"This could be messy," Loki warned as he reached for the door.

Tyr and Monkey King threw themselves aside. Very wise since sparks began to fly the moment his fingers brushed the white. This bit of perfection wasn't going to stop him from going inside. In fact . . . the mere existence of such a thing *annoyed* him.

He brushed his fingers across the surface, painting swirls of colors over the white. Those colors disappeared. He persisted;

no *thing* was going to prove itself stronger than him. He despised the emptiness of perfection, which had no place in life.

He was aware of a battle coming closer with the sounds of swords clashing and shouts. Had some of the other Norse gotten inside? Loki dared not look. He grabbed chaos and shoved his hand into the heart of the door, sending out waves of color in all directions.

When he was conscious again, Loki found Monkey King had thrown him over his bony shoulder and trotted along a line of cherry trees, all perfectly symmetrical, each bloom flawless --

"Put me down!"

"Conscious, eh?" He all but threw Loki to the ground.

Loki somehow landed on his feet and stayed there. His eyes blurred and the world moved in odd ways. Monkey King grabbed hold of his arm or else he would have fallen anyway.

"Damn," he whispered.

The word seemed to echo oddly around him and Monkey King gave a start at the sound.

"Curses are not allowed here," Monkey King said, frowning.

"Well, that's too *damned* bad."

Monkey King laughed, which also had an odd echo.

"So, neither good nor bad is allowed," Loki said. He grabbed at a branch and pulled off several flowers. The petals disappeared in his hand and reformed on the branch. "And nothing out of place."

"And yet here we are." Monkey King laughed with an expansive wave of his arm. "And we are most certainly out of place in the midst of such perfection."

Monkey King studied the tree beside him, his head tilted as he stared at the flowers, his eyes going unfocused, his face slack.

"Ah, no, my friend. Not what you want." Loki yanked him away.

He had not expected the reaction: Monkey King went from

a monk contemplating the perfection of a cherry blossom to a wild animal, cornered and attacking. Dagger teeth snapped straight at Loki's face and he leapt backwards, nearly losing his footing. Loki was not in shape for any kind of battle, physical or magical.

"Back!" Loki shouted.

Something registered in the creature's eyes and Monkey King's face changed again, going from wild animal to something more akin to -- but not quite -- human. He gave a little frown. "Now that was interesting," Monkey King said.

"Maybe from your side!" Loki took a deeper breath, one hand on the trunk of one of those too-perfect trees.

"For a moment . . ." Monkey King looked at the tree, his eyes narrowed. "For a moment I felt as though I could touch perfection and be a part of it; transcend the world we know and be part of something greater than vile creatures, tied forever to the whims of mankind. And then you tore me away from the perfection, which was not pleasant. However, I am grateful."

Loki nodded. He would be careful in the future.

"Red Coat and Tyr are holding off Chu Jong while the rest of the Norse attack from the rear. They followed Chu Jong in through the lesser door. Not a good symbolism to have them follow him. Chu Jong couldn't stop them, which helped to balance matters a little better."

"They didn't follow Chu Jong," Loki said with a lift of his head. "They followed *me*."

Monkey King stared for a moment and finally gave a whoop of laughter as something sublime changed in the feel of the battle. "Oh yes, oh yes! That changes perceptions entirely, does it not?"

"And for Gods, perception is everything." Loki glanced around the area, frowning. "Chu Jong wants to enforce perfection and this is the heart of his creation. But there is no perfection in real life. This is illusion."

"Illusion," Monkey King agreed. He bared his teeth in what might have been a smile. "Can we make these trees believe so?"

"We can start." Loki offered a smile of his own. "We are far stronger Gods than this two-bit scoundrel who has to use illusion to try to control the universe. Illusion will not work."

He pulled off a set of flowers. They crumbled and did not grow back.

"Perceptions," Monkey King said, "of the trees and of ourselves."

"And belief. We are made of equal parts of both, you know."

Shouts came from not far away. "Alas, I would love to have time to discuss such metaphysical subjects as the essence of the Gods, but I fear there are people coming to kill us."

"So little time for the finer points in life," Loki agreed.

And then the pack fell upon them. The few Norse fought against the many Chinese and he saw Tyr in the midst of the group, Odin and Thor to the rear. The mass of warriors surged into the perfect garden and began to do real damage as swords swung and magic rolled through the air.

Battle is always *chaos*, no matter how well-planned -- and this one wasn't planned at all, as the forces moved of their own will and power. Chu Jong had been tossing lines of perfectly dressed, synchronized warriors at them. Here, however, things worked differently. These were not soldiers but Gods against Gods. Some resorted to their primal powers. Loki watched the surging mass, feeling the power course through him.

Chu Jong, who stood apart from the battle, suddenly spun towards him. Oh, yes, Loki was a beacon of chaos in the midst of his perfection. Chu Jong started towards Loki, but Loki laughed and leapt into the heart of the battle.

No weapon, though. He ducked and kicked and he might have hit a few of his own people by mistake, but doing so added to the chaos, right? He let himself go and laughed as he dashed through the dozen fighters and out the other side.

To find himself beside Thor.

They both looked startled, but Loki laughed, gave Thor a little bow and kicked someone coming at them before Thor could get in a blow. He gave Loki a rather bemused shake of his head, so close to the old days that for a moment all the other problems from Ragnarok seemed to have disappeared. He could stand and fight by Thor again, in this time and place where old, lost wars no longer mattered.

"Destroy the trees!" Loki shouted, and the Norse obeyed, God and warrior, without question.

Chu Jong still had the home field advantage, so to speak. The Norse were outnumbered, which, more than anything, played against them. However, the Norse lived for the clash of arms. Their entire mythology revolved around battle and the old beliefs gave them an edge over the Chinese.

Tyr fell: a flash of light and he was gone to the darkness. The Norse felt the loss, their God of War destroyed in the midst of battle; Fenrir howled in distress and Torin gave a shout of dismay. The two of them leapt at the Chinese who had attacked Tyr and, since the enemy had weakened themselves in the battle, Fenrir and Torin had no trouble taking them. The enemy disappeared in their own flashes of light, but the Chinese hardly seemed to notice. Too many of them!

The Norse had to fight for every inch of the perfect land, cutting away at the trees, axes felling them left and right and again when they began to spring back up. This was not the battle the Norse most wanted to fight, but the trees would not stand before them.

He had not thought the war would focus on trees and perfection. Trees fell, grew, fell, grew . . . but Loki could tell the rule of three applied here because the third time, they did not regrow, or at least not as quickly. The damage slowed the

Chinese, as Loki directed the others into random -- one might even say chaotic -- movements through this pocket of perfection.

They began to make headway, though not fast enough. Dagur fell; a heartbeat of darkness overcame the battle as the Norse God of Day fell. He disappeared in another flash of light before the daylight returned. The Valkyrie called out in dismay, before they returned to the task of taking the chosen -- the mortal warriors -- to their reward. Centuries would pass before Dagur and Tyr were with the Norse again. It was no easy journey back from the emptiness.

Maybe, because he was so aligned with chaos, he felt the odd change before the others. Something powerful swept through the air and for a moment he thought all was lost. After a breath, the world settled and then was gone again -- and then back.

He went to his knees. Thor roared with anger and Loki blinked as he watched his former friend swing Mjuolnir and knock aside a half-dozen Chinese who had swept in, seeing him weakened. Red Coat and Monkey King leapt in to defend him as well while he fought this new attack --

Not an attack. A *change*.

Damn.

He struggled to his feet, taking in the battle with one quick glance. Chinese Gods had begun to look around the perfect orchard with distaste as Chu Jong's spell upon them unraveled. Chu Jong had been feeding this perfection to them like a drug; lotus eaters who drank in the very air of this place and fell under his control.

The Norse were freeing them, but too late . . . too late.

Everything began changing. The first tendrils of chaos, bright red and orange, swept in around them and he didn't think the others saw the danger. Loki reached out to grab hold of the miasmic power and use it.

He had to get their attention. Even those closest to him were not listening when he tried to shout. The din of the battle buried all else, a cacophony of sounds and movements threatening to overwhelm him.

He had to do something or all was lost.

Loki pulled the next wave of power into himself. The power burnt, but he captured what he could and sent the magic out in two waves. The first spread across the battlefield, knocking friend and foe alike to the ground.

He sent the second wave to the ceiling, tearing away the still hidden ceiling of the Imperial Palace and leaving them naked before P'an Ku. The supernova had already spread out in waves of fiery death, destroying everything within light-years. The magical covering around this world was all that kept them from their own deaths while pieces of P'an Ku's shell fell against the covering and flared like meteorites as they impacted. The sunlight was now a diffuse nebula, the swirling colors gorgeous and deadly.

"No time!" Loki shouted. "No time for this foolishness. We must push P'an Ku into his shell! I'm not ready to be one with chaos and I don't think any of you are, either. So now either we fight against each other and let the end take us, or else we work together and push P'an Ku back!"

A moment of indecision spread among the Chinese, many of whom might have been thinking about this for the first time.

"No!" Chu Jong shouted. "Let the great God come! Let him judge us!"

"Not before *we* judge you," Monkey King shouted. He ran, gamboling like an ape, through the wreckage of the orchard, but as he drew closer to Chu Jong, he rose up, taller than a human this time. Chu Jong started to back away, only to find Red Coat at his back. Everyone else stayed away from this drama, but Loki hoped this confrontation didn't go on for long. "You are a fool, Chu Jong. You tricked the others into siding with you and we could have forgiven you, in time. But you killed Di Jun, who was a wise God . . . and he was my friend. You murdered him for your own gain."

"He did not deserve to continue --"

He said no more. Monkey King yowled in wild, animal anger and leapt forward to attack. No one went to Chu Jong's aid. The screams didn't last long and, a moment later, the area brightened slightly and he was gone.

Monkey King shifted to human again, dispelling the blood on his hands and clothing with a sneer of disgust.

The trees withered and died. The building crumbled around them, while in the sky above something immense moved within the chaos. They were ants beneath his feet; he would take no notice of them. Chu Jong had been a fool to think he could ever have dealt with this being.

Loki felt confusion permeate the air. Had the death of Chu Jong and the break of his spell over his people left P'an Ku without true direction? If he had lost all connection --

"Time to end this!" Odin shouted, no doubt realizing what Loki did. Odin charged through the ruins of the Imperial Palace and out towards the welcome glow of Bifrost, outdistancing everyone else. The old rainbow path was the only hope they had of getting to P'an Ku, and even now it twisted and grew. Norse and Chinese, who had been fighting tooth and nail moments before, followed with battle yells of their own. Loki had followed as well, outstripping most of the others. Thor and Vali raced along the bridge to catch up with Odin, while the Ravens, returned to their old forms once more, fluttered about, dipping and sweeping -- Loki thought they might be uncertain of what to do and that made him stop as well.

Chinese Gods and lesser beings swarmed across Bifrost, rushing along the shimmering rainbow, with Red Coat and Monkey King in the lead of the second group. Loki could see the shape of the creature over them, not fully risen from its shell

--

Vali started past him, stopped. "I'm sorry."

And then he went on.

Loki gave a shout no less wild than the others. They had a chance! He darted along the curve, following the others --

And the Valkyrie swept down and surrounded him.

"Not this time, Loki." Freyja stopped before him, her arms held out to block the way. "This is not your time to sacrifice."

Fool that he was he tried to fight his way past her. The call of the battle sang in him and his blood boiled. He wanted to throw himself into the center of the maelstrom and didn't care if he came out the other side or not. The time after the battle didn't matter; it had never mattered to any of them.

He saw Torin and Fenrir heading past, ready to leap into the battle as well.

"No!"

He won past Freyja and Hildr, who didn't stop him this time because they knew he wasn't trying to reach Odin and the others. Instead, he tackled Torin and Fenrir and all three tumbled to the ground, a long hard fall. He hit and rolled, looking upward. For a moment he couldn't see or feel --

Chaos everywhere. They'd lost. Surely they'd lost --

The battle above him raged on, pieces of shell piercing the sky and creating craters around them. Storms battled against each other; wind and rain attacking the world, everything mixed with magic so powerful the mere touch would have seared the soul of any mortal who stood on this ground.

Loki had lost Torin and Fenrir in the maelstrom, but he didn't think they went to Bifrost again. The winds roared past and then, in a single breath, the powerful storm died. Somewhere nearby, Frigg gave a cry of fear and he felt a chill when he found her and the Queen of the West coming across the open ground. The chaos parted around them and Frigg lifted her arms and cried out in a voice that stilled all else for a moment:

"*The sea, storm-driven, seeks heaven itself. O'er the earth it flows, the air grows sterile; then follows the snows and the furious winds, for the Gods are doomed, and the end is death.*"

Even the chaos heard those ill-omened, prophetic words, and a moan swept through this nameless world where they had come to replay their parts one more time. Loki stared upward, feeling the pull --

Somewhere in the heavens above, Odin shouted in triumph and others joined in, the sound of their voices and the power of their existence spread out into a wall so dark that in a heartbeat Loki felt as though night came upon those below. The winds howled and, yes, they could have been on Earth in the wake of Ragnarok. Snow came in a white curtain, perhaps as a memory of the older battle. The ice followed on the wind and he felt the unnatural night chill him to his heart. Magic swept in and . . . died.

The stars came out. A jagged flicker of light flashed across the sky and dimmed, as though a crack had sealed. The warriors began to appear on Bifrost, one after another.

Loki stared, waiting, waiting--

But Odin didn't return.

CHAPTER THIRTY-SIX

The Queen of the West stood with a hand on Frigg's shoulder, staring into the sky, though she couldn't say what they watched now that the battle was over. "It is done, Lady."

Frigg bowed her head, letting the loss and the sorrow come. How odd, the Queen of the West thought, because she held no such attachments. She moved in accordance with the flow of the universe and never a tie . . . except for the faithful white tiger, ever at her side. What sorrow would she have felt if he had disappeared into the abyss with the others?

She felt nothing for the loss of Chu Jong, who had been a tool she had let get out of hand because she had no way to judge emotions. She had thought him a God, akin to herself -- oh, not quite, of course, but more akin to her than to the ghost troops he controlled. She didn't understand why Frigg wept for the loss of Odin and the others.

"They'll be back, you know," she said, uncertain of the protocols.

Frigg lifted her head, tears leaving sparkling paths down her face and falling like jewels frozen in the icy storm that over took them. Loki looked to her, pain in his face as well.

"He and I have been together forever," Frigg whispered, the words nearly lost as the storm howled with loss the northern Gods felt. "And though he will be back, it will be a different time, a different place. I shall search for him in my runes. But, until then, Odin is no more."

Loki, the one who was not -- and was -- one of them, reached out and gently put a hand on Frigg's arm, offering comfort unspoken.   Her sorrow mirrored in his dark eyes where the Queen of the West had not expected to see such regrets.

And for a moment, oh, how the Queen of the West envied the little Norse Goddess who had such connections with others.

She'd never envied anyone before and she felt confused. A few Chinese gathered nearby, looking around with shock and dismay as though they had finally awakened from a nightmare. She'd helped Chu Jong control them and their loss now was, at least in part, her fault.

She had never felt guilty before, either.

Emotions came like a disease spread from the Norse. Dangerous creatures. She had not realized until now, until too late; she had changed in the moment when she looked upon the tears of the Goddess from the north.

Changed and there was no going back. She walked away, back to the Chinese who fell to the ground and bowed before her.

"Come, my children, come. We must rebuild now."

Where the grand palace had stood, she raised a small but lovely building, surrounded by gardens, blooming and inviting despite the dark of the night. A gate marked the way to the west with jasmine twining around it. Not her sort of place, really -- this was a summer world -- and, yet, welcome. Change. Maybe this was what she took from this fiasco. Change and progress, which had never seemed important to her before.

She patted the tiger on the head. He cast one half-snarl at the wolf, but walked on with her to the gate. Red Coat and Monkey King came to greet her.

A lovely little place.

It would grow.

CHAPTER THIRTY-SEVEN

The shell had fallen back. P'an Ku had not expected the pressure and had stopped moving.

Tenacious little beings, even those with more power than the others, throwing themselves at him. He let the shell fall closer around him, feeling the peace and comfort return. Better here?

A voice whispered nearby, something akin to him and not.

Rest a while, Elder Brother. Let the universe go its own way a while longer. I am sorry she awoke you.

He listened to this odd, subtle thing, which was both God and wild, this Monkey King. He found wisdom in the strange creature's thoughts. He also found love for the chaotic and unexpected. Nature could not be driven by rules. Humanity and humanity's Gods were all born of the same nature and universe P'an Ku had first set in motion. They were his creations after all because he had created the parameters within which they existed.

Something to think about. Something to consider.

So he curled up within his shell . . . and let the universe go on for a while yet. Days, weeks, months, years, centuries, eons -- time meant nothing to him. He would rise again at another age to see what wonders these humans might have made by then.

Chapter Thirty-Eight

L oki led the survivors up Bifrost towards the ship, trying not to falter as they followed him. Odin had always led them back to *Asgard* and this was not the position Loki wanted. However, someone needed to get them away from this world and the Chinese before trouble broke out again. They had no reason left to fight, but a conflict might start anyway. Their emotions were still too high and the battle always called to them.

They lost too much. And though he knew Odin would come back, he would rather not have lost him and seen the pain in Frigg's face. He knew they had also lost Mani, Delling, Eostre . . . and Vali. He wasn't certain which others were gone. Loki had tried to bury his fears and overcome the unexpected grief. Now, almost to the clouds, he glanced behind him to measure other losses . . . and found something that stopped him there, part way to *Asgard*.

Baldr walked at his back.

"What the hell are you doing here?" Loki demanded. The others, who hadn't been very close, backed away, leaving this to him. He would have thought someone would have dealt with Baldr during the battle -- but he realized he hadn't seen Baldr in the heat of the fight, only when he'd had a chance to attack from behind. The rest of the fight had probably been too *uncivilized* for him.

Baldr gave an unexpected smile, as though he could not see the anger in Loki and the others or understand why anything should be amiss. "We are the same, you know, Loki. You're not like the others, either."

"I was *never* like the others, but that made no difference before you created the rift. You betrayed us, both then and now. You think I'm going to trust you?"

Baldr lifted a hand to wave those words away. Thor arrived, though he stopped a few steps away. His face grew livid with rage and, for once, the anger was not directed at Loki. Baldr, though, seemed blissfully unaware of any ill-will towards him.

"It's long past time I came home to my true heritage," Baldr continued and waved his hand towards *Asgard* this time. "The times have changed and the Norse need someone who stepped away from the dark past long ago. Odin is gone, you know. It's time I took charge. I am his son."

"So is Thor," Loki said.

Baldr laughed. "He's a brute. Even the Norse can't want his kind to lead them any longer. Look where it took them!"

Thor took a step forward, but Loki shook his head. He wasn't certain why, but the warning worked. Thor waited, but his hand had gone to the hammer resting in the belt at his side.

"You are the one who directed the Chinese into this war against us," Loki reminded Baldr, trying, he realized, to see some logic in what Baldr thought.

Baldr gave the little wave of his hand once more. Loki saw no connection with reality. "You need an experienced hand. I've returned to lead the Norse to a brighter, better and more civilized age."

He heard Freyja hiss in anger and Thor had Mjuolnir in hand now, his displeasure replaced by determined, and barely controlled, rage. Loki realized they were fast heading into another battle if something wasn't settled quickly.

"We can't stand here forever, Loki --"

"Sometimes you can't go home, Baldr, and you aren't going with us. In fact, I wish you would . . . go to Hel."

Loki drew magic into the shape of a sword and stabbed straight through Baldr's black heart. Baldr went to his knees in surprise and shock. Not dead -- not gone too quickly as he tried to grab magic to save himself.

Loki saw shock in the faces of the others, though Frigg nodded. Or perhaps this was the end of some vision, finally come fully into play.

"You blamed me for his death," Loki reminded them, looking at the others. Some bowed their heads and didn't meet his eyes. "And now I fulfill the myth at last. And none too soon, I think."

"*Would you know yet more?*" Frigg asked, her voice echoing on the wind.

He shivered. "No. No more. Not now. Let us at least pretend we have free will for a while yet."

She bowed her head and he wondered, suddenly, if she read the runes . . . or if she controlled them.

A foul wind rose out of the east and with it a keening scream. At another time, the scream had been associated with the banshee -- the bane sidhe and the sound of death. Most of the Norse hurried past the body with hardly a glance, but Loki stayed to see the end. He didn't fear his daughter. Thor remained as well, watching to mark the end.

Hel arrived with her darkest minions, creatures starved for a taste of life. The body had not yet fallen, though the spirit only hung on with a fine misty light, bright in some places, but oh so dark in others. He supposed his own soul looked much the same.

The Valkyrie swept down from the skies but they stood at Loki's back. They would not be taking Baldr to a different reward; certainly not to Valhalla to feast and wait for the next great battle, nor even to Freyja's Fields and a quieter afterlife. He wouldn't even go where the other Gods had gone. Not yet. Loki had cast a curse he'd built upon for centuries and had given the result to Baldr rather than Thor.

Oh, but Baldr would be back. The Gods always returned. Maybe, though, something would change the next time.

The keening rose to a screaming pitch and darkness spread in a cloud of death. Hel and the Valkyrie held the miasmic force away from Loki and the others and finally the cloud of dark malice left on the wind. Hel alone remained behind and gave her father a bow of her head before she took to the air and disappeared as well.

The cold returned as Baldr's body disappeared with a flickering sputter rather than a glow, lost to the universe, transported to wherever Hel took him, waiting to be remade again. He would be a problem for later.

Thor gave a nod of appreciation for what Loki had done. Loki had never been slow to do something that needed done for the betterment of the group.

"You should have come to me," he said to Thor. "You should have trusted me to handle Baldr the first time."

Thor bowed his head and went past.

Loki watched where the Chinese had already started building a new beginning, there on the world which had survived the disaster. He could see Red Coat sitting on a bridge by a pond and the irreverent Monkey King climbing to the roof of the new building.

Loki headed towards *Asgard*. He wasn't certain who followed him or if they had decided he'd gone too far. He didn't care. The deed was done and he was glad enough to have taken Baldr out of the picture.

Thor waited at the doorway to *Asgard*, the Ravens at his back. Torin and Fenrir were there as well and a weight lifted from Loki's heart that he'd been afraid to name before now.

"I wish things could have been different," Thor finally admitted. "I wish a lot of things could have been."

He stepped aside, letting Loki go in ahead of him. Loki had never noticed how much Thor resembled his father.

Stepping inside felt, finally, like coming home, although *Asgard* seemed dull without Odin and Tyr. Too much had been lost in the battle. He paused inside the airlock and watched the two who followed him. Torin glanced at Thor and gave Loki a weary nod.

"Thor, I think you need to meet your son, Torin," Loki said.

Thor turned to him with eyes wide in shock. More surprised, Loki thought, than when he had killed Baldr. Had he even surprised Frigg?

"I don't understand." Thor looked at the boy with shock and respect. Torin had been tested in battle, after all, and stood the line with the Norse Gods. Thor gave a bewildered shake of his head. "Why did you raise him? Why did you treat him so well after all I had done to you?"

Loki gave a little laugh, surprising himself. "I thought I raised him to be everything you despised. But, really, I think I was only keeping him safe."

Torin laughed as well.

"I'm weary," Loki admitted. "I want to return to the station now. I think we've had enough of each other's company for a while, don't you think?"

"Rest," Thor agreed. "I'll take you home. I'll hold to his promise."

Loki started down the hall, all too aware of the Ravens following *him*.

CHAPTER THIRTY-NINE

Torin had somehow found his room on *Asgard*. Or maybe not -- maybe the room had simply reformed for him and appeared where he expected the room to appear. He'd never dealt with so much magic before. He was getting a feel for how the powers worked, though. He wished he had asked a few more questions when he'd had the chance.

He missed Tyr, who had helped him get settled in.

Odin was gone. Torin had trouble understanding the depth of the concept. Odin had always been a part of his world, though he had never met his grandfather until this journey. He wished he could have known him on a personal level, but maybe they would have the chance the next time.

He had trouble dealing with the idea of forever. He tried to observe the effects in Loki, Sigyn and now Thor. He wanted to figure out his place in this madness.

Someone knocked on the door. He keyed it open from the desk and Fenrir looked in, alone this time. Torin suspected Hel had her hands full right now. He tried not to shiver at the thought.

"Come in," he said with a wave. He ached from the battle and didn't want formality tonight.

Fenrir must have felt the same way. He crossed the room eased himself into the chair close to the desk with a slight wince.

"Long time since a real battle," he admitted and gave a painful shrug. "And I learned I didn't enjoy war as well as I thought I would. Is this maturity?"

"Are you asking this of the youngest person on this ship?" Fenrir smiled, a flash of sharp teeth.

"What is going to happen now?" Torin asked, leaning forward. "Everything is different, isn't it?"

"Yes. And long past time things should have changed. We kept clinging to what we had been and I think this may have been part of what brought us to this place. We yearned for another epic battle. The battle was all we lived for -- so maybe we had our hand in awakening P'an Ku as well as the Chinese."

"Loki isn't going to go looking for trouble," Torin offered. He had seen the Ravens following Loki and knew this meant a change in who headed the pantheon now.

"He won't look, but trouble will find him. Still, I think things will be different." He looked around the room. "I have never dealt much with technology, but it fascinates me."

"And I've rarely had my hand on much magic."

"I think I see different futures for us."

CHAPTER FORTY

R ed Coat found Monkey King in the place he least expected to see him. His friend sat on the edge of the bridge, his toes dipping into the water below, the koi dancing around in delight as he showered them with crumbs of bread. He had never seen Monkey King so serene before and he thought to leave him to peace.

"Sit with me," Monkey King said without looking. "I could use the company. The fish don't say much, do they?"

"That is part of their charm."

Monkey King gave a snort of a laugh, seeming more himself for a moment. "Well, the battle is all done. What sort of trouble can we get into now?"

Red Coat settled beside him and dropped his own bread into the water where ecstatic, and soon-to-be-very-fat, koi danced around in a delightful swirl of colors.

"It seems to me," Red Coat said with a tilt of his head, "that Loki promised us apples. I think we should consider how we will collect on his promised gift."

Monkey King grinned with delight. "We need a ship, which will take a while to prepare. The two of us can sail the stars and bring trouble where we may."

"I think the Queen of the West will be glad to see us go, too," Red Coat agreed. "Yes, time for us to move on and see this universe we saved."

"And get apples from Loki."

"I'm sure he'll be pleased to see us."

And they both laughed with delight.

CHAPTER FORTY-ONE

S igyn blinked back tears of joy and disbelief as she met them at the bay, breathless after the run from *Chaos*. She looked to Loki and the Ravens standing at his shoulders, her eyes going wide with surprise.

"Things have changed," Loki said with a sigh.

"Then *he* is gone." Her voice was an awed whisper mixed with loss. Odin had always been a part of their life, even when he wasn't nearby. He had already been reborn by the time they'd returned the first time. Loki understood her feeling of loss. "I felt him go, you know. We were monitoring the area, expecting the nova to spread. I felt the change long before news reached us about how the star had unexpectedly collapsed and stabilized. But he is gone?"

"For a while. I'm not certain how I inherited the terrible two, but I seem to be stuck with them."

Both Ravens grinned, a show of bright teeth. He could hear them whisper to him now and then, imparting knowledge and distracting him. He couldn't begin to parse most of what he heard. No matter. They would work together.

Sigyn took a deeper breath and nodded.

"I'm going with Thor for a while," Torin told her, sparing Loki from saying those words. "I'll be back, though. I promise."

She looked at Thor, her eyes narrowed with murderous

rage. Loki touched her arm, drawing her attention. "That old tale is done, my love. Now we need to let go and start something new. I have the Ravens; I am the leader of the Norse Pantheon for a while. I think this is the time for a change."

"I think Torin and I better get out of here before Loki decides to see what changes he can make in us," Thor said with a bit of a grin.

"I would not dream of it," Loki replied.

"And, oh, how he lies," Thor said, but laughed this time. "We'll meet again. Maybe over some wine instead of ale."

Thor gave a proper bow to Sigyn and hurried back to the ship which sat shimmering in the pale light of the bay. They had agreed Thor should take *Asgard* and find his own path for a while, out from under both Odin and the lies he'd lived. The others, who would not have felt safe away from *Asgard*, would go with him. They would answer to Loki, though. No matter how far the ship went, they would feel their connection to him.

Torin paused before embracing Sigyn and whispering in her ear. She gave a tentative smile and a nod of farewell, brushing a tear from her cheek. She had, after all, raised him as her own son.

"I have much to learn and so does he," Torin said. He followed his father who stood by the ship's oh-so-normal airlock.

Loki watched the two disappearing into *Asgard* and the world of magic. Despite his new position, he wanted nothing more than to go home to Sigyn and *Chaos*. They all needed time to adjust. Besides, if what Frigg suspected, but hadn't seen clearly, proved to be true -- they'd be working together soon. She told him something dark waited out there. Dangerous. If they were lucky, the dark would stay away.

He wasn't feeling particularly lucky these days.

Another person appeared at the airlock and walked towards them, head down, looking from side to side. Fenrir had never been comfortable in civilization and yet --

"I want to stay a while." He looked to Loki with a touch of worry, his brows furrowed. "I want to know the other side, Loki. I want to understand Torin's world."

Loki glanced at Sigyn, but she had already put a hand on Fenrir's arm. "There are wonders here. You'll enjoy the adventure, at least for a while."

So a new order, long overdue, had begun. Odin had held to the past. Loki wasn't going to look for another Ragnarok, but he suspected trouble would find them anyway.

The End

###

Author's Notes: Would you know yet more?

Anyone who is familiar with Norse Mythology will be either amused or appalled by the liberties I took with the original myths. I am not an expert in Norse mythology, but through several years of writing, rewriting and editing, I did a considerable amount of research. I knew what I wanted to do and I tied as much as I could to the original myths before I twisted everything into something different.

Would you know yet more? This is a line taken directly from the *Poetic Edda*, a collection of Norse mythology, most in bits and pieces, but enough to have some interesting background material to work with. I read two ebook versions of the *Poetic Edda* -- not the easiest way to read such a work with the notes spread out all over -- but helpful enough for what I wanted. (*The Poetic Edda*, Nook Book Format, ISBN: 204-0-011-806-06-3 and 294-0-023-162-44-7. Both are translations by Henry Adams Bellows)

I read several other helpful books. *Medieval Epics and Sagas* (Borders Classics, ISBN: 978-1-58726-276-0). While the book didn't cover the material from this book, it did provide more of the feel for the northern mythology.

The Norse Myth by Kevin Crossley Holland (Pantheon Books, ISBN: 978-0-394-748-46-7) is a far more accessible way to read the material from the Poetic Edda and clarified a few of the problems I'd had reading through the ebook versions. However, for my own purpose, digging the material out of the ebook proved to be a lot more rewarding, like finding treasures hidden away in an intricate maze.

Norse Mythology by John Lindow (Oxford University Press, ISBN: 978-0-19-515328-8) was by far the most helpful book overall. This wonderful paperback is an encyclopedic collection of information on Gods, Heroes, Rituals and Beliefs. The amount of information in this book is fantastic and I found it difficult to look through and not get ideas for more things to write.

Why are there no Kennings in the novel? Kennings were special nicknames for just about everything in Old Norse. I had intended to use them in this book, but I quickly discovered they made everything more complicated and difficult to read for those who were not familiar with the idea of kennings. Since I don't expect this book to be popular with Norse historians, I decided to leave the kennings off.

You might want to look into them, though. They're fascinating. (http://en.wikipedia.org/wiki/List_of_kennings)

I spent a lot of time surfing through Internet pages, finding odd bits and pieces of information. Because I planned to purposefully change the story, I didn't have to worry about the authenticity of some of the material. On the other hand, I spent time with my various sets of Encyclopedias, too -- so things probably balanced out.

What about the Chinese?

Two books gave me considerable insight into and information about the Chinese Gods and myths. The first is *Myths and Legends of China* by E. T. C. Werner (Dover, 0486-28092-6) which is a very good introduction to the complexity of Chinese mythology. The second book is the lovely *Chinese Fairy Tales & Fantasies*, translated and edited by Moss Roberts (Pantheon Books, 0-394-73994-9), which is where I found the wonderful one-paragraph tale, *The Tiger Behind the Fox*.

Since the story doesn't often deal with the past of the Chinese Gods, I didn't need the same level of research, but I spent days going over the material. Learning anything is fun and you never know when something you find might be useful elsewhere.

There are always more tales to tell.

About the Author:

Hello!

I am an eclectic and prolific author whose has published in a number of genres, including young adult mystery, urban fantasy, epic fantasy and science fiction as well as nonfiction books on writing. While I started on the outer edges of traditional publication with sales to small press and magazines publishers, I have since moved most of my work to the indie realm and I am madly in love with the new world of publishing and the direct contact with readers.

I live in Nebraska with my husband, my cats and a small but entirely useless dog.

I also own Forward Motion for Writers and the ezine, Vision: A Resource for Writers.

Connect with Zette:

Web Site: http://lazette.net

Twitter: http://twitter.com/lazetteg

Facebook: http://www.faccbook.com/lazette.gifford

Facebook Author Page: Facebook:

https://www.facebook.com/pages/Lazette-Gifford/352371884942342

Joyously Prolific Blog: http://zette.blogspot.com/

Email: zette@lazette.net

The following pages contain previews to two soon-to-be-released print books. I hope you enjoy them! They are also available in ebook format from both Amazon and Smashwords.

Preview: Paid in Gold and Blood

Chapter One

At Silver Pass the snow had settled knee deep except where others had trudged through and flattened it to mud and ice. The frigid wind swept over the white-capped mountains and felt like the cold hand of death itself. Katashan pulled his heavy cloak closer and tried not to feel the bone-aching chill. Emista himself, the old God of Ice, could still rule in a place like this where summer probably never reached.

In a few more steps he topped the crest of the high mountain pass and there Katashan stopped and stared at the distant golden shore and sapphire sea far below. He waited for a feeling elation at seeing the end of his five month journey and the new future the distant view promised.

Unfortunately, he'd already wearied of too many new beginnings in his life. He couldn't look at the sparkling sea and the land of Cyrenia and believe they promised him any better life than what he'd already given up: the good and the bad, and all of it lost to him now.

The windswept silence suddenly filled with the bray of donkeys and the inharmonious yell of the caravan master. The rest of Katashan's traveling companions would soon make their way up the trail to this final pass along the Old Iron Road. Tyren, the shaggy and unkempt caravan master, had a voice that could wake the dead. As far as Katashan could tell it had no effect whatsoever on either the thirty donkeys or the half dozen workers in his employ.

Tyren had been an odd companion for someone who had

spent a few years serving in the temples of home. The caravan master believed in every omen and superstition, while at the same time he cursed gods and men alike. It had made a very long, and loud, journey.

Tyren did have his virtues, though. The man knew every trail, village and ford between Taris and Cyrenia. He also had no problem taking hire from a northerner, even though Katashan might be unpopular where they traveled. The war between Cyrenia and Taris had ended only three short years before and trouble still erupted along the border now and then.

Katashan had hurried ahead of the caravan to do more than gawk at the welcoming sight of the Inner Sea. Stone-carved Verina Guardians -- waist high images of the kneeling goddess -- stood sentinel at every important locality along the Iron Road. The statues represented an old religion which was now in abeyance in the south and had been since the old Taris Empire fell into smaller, and often warring, kingdoms.

Katashan hadn't realized he could feel any affection for the Gods who had turned their backs on him when he needed them most. Yet the first time he had seen the kneeling statue of Verina, protector of travelers, he'd felt an odd stirring in his heart. During the long journey he had stopped at every Verina statue and made a token offering of food or drink. He had served in her temple for a few years when he was younger. Those days seemed so long ago now, that it might have been another person who had prayed at the altars and wished all travelers in the world peace and safety.

A shame those prayers had never been saved for himself.

Tyren and his men had scoffed at the superstitious northerner at first, but as the journey progressed with few problems, he saw Tyren eyeing the old goddess with some consideration. It amused Kastashan to think he may have helped to reintroduce a piece of the old religion to counter the apostasy of the south, where the Cyrenian monarchy had introduced new gods as soon as they broke allegiance with Taris.

"Up! Up ye' damned beasts!" Tyren bellowed and the donkeys answered in much the same tone. Soon the pack would catch up with him. After so many months on the trail, Katashan knew better than to waste the few precious moments he had to himself.

However, even knowing where to look, he still had trouble finding the Verina Guardian for this pass. He had started to believe that being this close to the Cyrenian heartland, it had been thrown down during the war.

He spotted the very top of the statue's head showing through a snowdrift off to the right, farther from the trail than he had expected. By then he could also hear the plodding step of the lead donkeys and knew he didn't have much time if he wanted a moment to say his thanks in private for having had such a trouble-free journey.

Getting to the statue wasn't easy this time as he plowed through the snow more than knee deep in many places. He tried not to curse as he forced his way through the ice crusted snowdrifts. Katashan had always believed the Gods listened at the worst of times, and he had already dared their ire too often in the past to take a chance now. He even bit back a curse when his foot caught on a snow covered limb that sent him sprawling at the feet of the Guardian.

Katashan stood and quickly brushed snow from his pants and cloak. Tyren had almost topped the rise, all but dragging the lead donkey with him. Katashan took the last step and reached out, brushing snow from the covered statue --

The stone felt uncommonly warm and should have melted the snow for several feet around the shrine if this had been true warmth. What he felt was magic and that could not be good.

"There you be," Tyren said from behind him. "Why'd ya not take the cleared path to your Guardian? Never struck me as a snow lover."

Path? Katashan turned and could clearly see the stone-lined trail a few steps to his left. He could not possibly have missed the path before, except that the Goddess intended him to trample through the snow.

And even fall as he had.

She would not have done this on a whim. The Gods had never shown a taste for burlesque before, though irony and farce seemed common enough. So why send --

"Damn," he whispered despite himself.

Katashan quickly retraced the steps to where he had fallen. He knelt, ignoring the cold, and brushed snow away from the limb . . . and found frozen cloth beneath the ice and then fingers, blue as the ocean below.

"What norther ritual is it this time?" Tyren demanded as the rest of the caravan began to move past, his men anxiously herding the laden donkeys onward.

"Tether the animals and bring a blanket," Katashan ordered. He looked up into Tyren's scowling face. "I've found a body."

Preview -- Xenation: Draw the Line

Chapter One

Morgan Michael Doreet had prepared himself *not* to be impressed with the station, despite his appointment as the head of the science team stationed there. He'd read everything he could about the place, from the first reports (when most of the news teams dismissed the find as an elaborate hoax) to the last reports sent a couple months ago by the science team based on the station. The surprise of finding an abandoned alien space station had given way to annoyed frustration. The station remained, for the most part, closed to the science teams. Everyone lived in the only area accessible, a small band along the edge, while the station kept its secrets behind impenetrable walls.

Oh, there were still interesting *things* to be found on the station anyway. If nothing else, the company proved odd enough. In the narrow habitable area, the station accommodated humans, Norishi, Ksa and even a few Click. The station brought together four alien races who normally wouldn't live in such close proximity even though they shared an affinity in habitats. That they had all taken up residence to study the station seemed far more noteworthy than the scanty reports on the makeup of the station's structure.

Soft bells chimed with just enough sound to draw attention as the captain announced they were coming off slide into real space. Morgan leaned forward, waiting for the first glimpse of his new home, this place at the edge of exploration where humans went to see what they could find, because curiosity was their worst -- and best -- trait.

The *Blue Star* came out of slide, slipping nicely from the path of dull red and bright yellow and into the cold darkness of real space again. The pilot had a good touch without any of the sudden drop-and-lurch back to reality that he'd felt on the last craft. They arrived relatively close to the station, there not being much of a gravity well to worry about here. Morgan stood on the View Deck and blinked as real space came into focus.

The station looked blocky, which was not the shape a space station should be by human standards. He caught a hint of grayish-green color from the glowing surface, the light created by self-rejuvenating phosphorescent bacteria in the walls; he read those reports. Altogether, the station appeared dull and unpretentious despite its unusual origins.

Then he began to realize the *size*. Not just know the abstract numbers in a report, but to actually comprehend what those numbers meant. The small glowing bubbles he barely saw at this distance were grow-domes tethered to the larger station. Each one held one hundred acres of land but they looked like peas set against the edge of the station.

While Morgan tried to accept what he saw, he noticed a movement off to the left. While he watched, a huge dark block of the station rose, narrowed, turned and rebuilt itself near the area where humans, Norisha, Ksa and Click lived.

Seeing the station -- truly comprehending the size, power and *alieness* -- finally took his breath away. Xeno Station, or Xenation as the people stationed here called the place, turned out to be far more impressive than he had expected. Frighteningly so for the man who came to take over the science section. People back on Mars expected him to find answers.

One of the *Blue Star* crew in a neat grey and blue uniform stepped up beside him, stared for a moment, and then shook her head. Yellow and blue curls bounced up and down and her dark face creased with a look of trepidation.

"There's been a lot of changes since the last time we were

here, half a year ago," she said. "More blocks out here towards the edge. Maybe that means the station is going to open new areas?"

"Maybe," he said, and wondered if he should hope so. New areas would be an important coup for him when he took over from Samplin, who had resigned to go back home. Samplin would be leaving with the *Blue Star* in a couple days. This was going to be a quick changeover, but that didn't worry Morgan. "Have you seen the station make this kind of change before?"

"This is the second time I've seen it happen." She frowned, leaning closer to the screen, her thin arms resting on the bar that ran across this side of the long, narrow room. This wasn't really a window, but they did a damned good job of making it look like one. "I've made six trips in the last four years. I don't know. Just looks like the place has been more active since the last time. A lot more bulges, a lot more blocks. I don't know if I like it."

She gave one last shake of her head and headed away. He tried not to let her attitude worry him.

Morgan remained to watch through the rest of the approach. The ship headed inwards on a slight curve and didn't noticeably slow until they reached the grow domes: bubble-topped and crowned with solar panels, they captured ambient light from the distant bright blue star that claimed this system. The domes stayed tethered to the bulk of the station by long filaments of bonding cords which snaked their way through the dark, glittering with the trace lights to keep the few craft from snaring them. They made a pretty spider web of tiny stars. Part of the dome had a clear covering allowing for the capture of even more of the ambient energy and making the enclosures into self-sustaining eco-systems. As the *Blue Star* went by, he had a close hand view of what looked like a wheat field, the stalks waving slightly in an artificially created wind. A little farther on workers swarmed over an infrastructure, putting together another dome to help support the expanding human population. So far, the other three races seemed content to have their food imported, but humans liked to be self-sufficient wherever they went.

Morgan saw movement to the right and caught a glimpse of a greenish Click ship leaping out from the station like a small round ball tossed aside by a giant. In the next breath the craft darted into slide drive so quickly his breath caught, expecting an explosion and disaster. Instead he only saw a little flash of red as the ship disappeared onto the slide path.

Another thing he'd read about but never actually seen.

Almost immediately, a long thin Norishi ship pulled out from a dock to the left and lower down. He watched as the craft moved past; jet-black, arrow-shape, and without a show of any of the weapons for which the Norishi were so well known. He wished the Norishi hadn't made a base at Xenation, but the aliens appeared determined to make certain of their presence wherever humans and Ksa settled.

Which, from all he could tell, was very odd since the Norishi apparently hated all races but their own. The Norishi had secrets, too. In all the contacts, both friendly and unfriendly, not a single male had been spotted, even though the females appeared to be very close to human females in appearance and in biology. At least that was the rumor, since no one admitted to doing a real examination of one of the dead. Such an admission could start an interstellar war, and the Norishi were trouble enough already. They relied on scans, which were unfortunately calibrated for humans, so might be missing something important.

Morgan would much rather not have them around. They complicated matters in an already unstable situation, a place where everyone dealt with far too much politics, which he generally detested, whether alien or human.

"Two minutes to docking. Please go to the nearest seating."

Morgan gave one last glance to the screen and crossed to the seats where he still had a good view of the station as they moved closer. The other passengers were apparently holed up in their suites, but he'd wanted more than the small computer screen view when he arrived. This would be home, though he couldn't say for how long.

Morgan felt the maneuvering jets fire and saw the ship's angle change slightly so they ran with their side to the ship, leaving him with a view along the edge, staring out at a far distant star and the faint trail of a comet, barely visible to the eye. Debris of all sorts littered the area around the station, giving rise to speculation about a planetary system that might have been here once. Some suggested a very old and devastating war had torn apart the worlds, though no one had found signs of any sort of battle.

Who knew what secrets Xenation still held?

Morgan saw a slight ripple of movement along the station wall, followed by a slight bump before they stopped. He had expected something far more violent since they were not matching speed to a spinning station like they would have with anything human. Instead, the station itself caught and held them, somehow bleeding off acceleration from one heartbeat to the next. They came to a gentle stop.

Damn, if they could get their hands on any of the technology that ran this station --

Which, of course, was a big part of his job. People back at the Inner Worlds Council wanted at least some of the power represented by this station, but they were getting wise enough to know they couldn't walk in and grab a few things. Samplin had come in with that attitude and now he gladly let the position go to someone else.

Nearly everyone who came to Xenation expected to make

their name and fortune here. In some ways, Morgan felt the same way. He wanted to believe he would be the one to break open the secrets, explore farther into the station, and come out again with the answers.

However, he really took the position because this was an unusual place and far from the crowds on the Inner Worlds and the continual oversight of politically-connected supervisors who wanted findings to coincide with whatever pet theory they wanted to promote. Xenation would give him peace to study the station itself, and time to work on other projects as well.

He didn't need to worry about the politics here. He had known Station Master Neva NiGwen for years before Neva and Ashur, her late husband, came in the first wave of humans to settle and explore the station. Morgan knew he could work with her.

The captain announced they had docked and people could now leave the ship. Morgan had been staring at the side of the station where swirls of bacteria brightened and faded. He reluctantly left the view and went back to his room where he gathered up his personal bag. The few other crates would be sent out by the crew. There were a dozen other passengers on the small ship, but he was the only one stopping here permanently. He had only met a few of others in passing because he'd tied himself to a computer and studied every Xenation report he'd grabbed back on Earth before being shipped here. This wasn't where he had expected to be going and he hadn't been prepared.

Two months in transit had helped. He'd read everything four times over. He could have written a book on Xenation by now, without ever setting foot on it.

However. . . .

The more he read the reports, the more he had felt as though *something* was missing. The reports seemed to lack the enthusiasm he would have expected in an endeavor of this kind, even given some of the frustrations. He'd worked on newly settled colonies a few times, and he saw none of the same reactions here.

He appeared to be the last of the passengers heading out, the others to spend a few hours wandering the strange station. The captain, a short pleasant man, stood by the door as everyone left, a nice service, not often seen on the smaller craft running out on the edge of humanity's turf. The double doors of the airlock stood open, but he could see little except a distant wall beyond. There was already a difference in the air on the ship as it took in the atmosphere from Xenation.

"Welcome to your new home, Etech Doreet. I assume you are not trying to carry a powered weapon of any sort onto the station?"

"No, I'm not. I know better. Do people still try?"

"Just removed two laser pistols from the group ahead of you," Captain Ness said with a nod towards the open airlock doors. "I didn't expect you to be that stupid, but I'm required to ask."

"Have you ever had someone get past you?" he asked, pausing even though he was anxious to see the station.

"Not me. Did talk to one Captain a couple years ago who let someone through. He had to stop making the run. The station won't let the ship dock anymore. I don't want to take that chance."

He'd heard of that happening with ships, but hadn't been sure he believed it until now. There were enough odd rumors about Xenation that it was hard to tell the real from the imagined. This truth pointed to the station having considerable intelligence. He held back a shiver and looked out at the shadowed area beyond again.

"Is this a profitable run?" he asked.

"Better than most out here." He gave a bright smile. "This is the only place a free trader can have direct contact with the

Ksa and Click. We don't pick up much, but any little item can bring a profit."

"And the Norishi?"

"We don't deal with the Norishi," he said. "Or rather, they won't deal with us. We have gotten a couple things, but only through the Ksa. And everything approved through the Station Master, by the way. They have a great open market here."

He nodded, but his attention had finally turned to the area beyond the airlock. Xenation was already a place steeped in mythology. He was a modern day Shaman, come to see if he could make connection with the powers of the past.

"Good luck with your work, Etech."

"Thank you." He pulled the strap of his bag up over his shoulder, and headed out of the airlock.

The first thing he noticed was what he often did on new worlds: the taste of the air. He had the full feel of it now that he was outside the *Blue Star*. Most stations had a filtered taste, either good or bad depending on how well the system worked. Stepping from the ship to the station brought something entirely unexpected. The air had a slight taste like unripe green apples. Not unpleasant, at least.

Then he noticed that the docks, unlike those on any other station he'd visited, were not bitterly cold. The gravity was no problem, either. The *Blue Star* had been adjusting the gravity to match Xenation's since they left the last port, so he felt comfortable walking here.

Lights hung on tall poles and illuminated the area in intersecting circles on the metal floor, but still left the very high ceiling lost in shadows. Spots glowed on the dark walls in both bright and muted colors as though a rainbow had spattered itself across the area. Self-sustaining bacteria, he reminded himself. Some of it glowed in spectrums humans couldn't see.

Just bacteria. Just light. But damn, the pattern looked like art to him; and like many others who had stepped into the station, he felt a whisper of kinship between humans and the long-gone aliens who had built Xenation. The colors made him feel oddly comfortable.

For the most part, the station was built of normal materials, though and the metals had plainly been mined from the system. Humans did the same thing when they built their own stations.

Something squeaked and bounded towards him. Morgan stepped back in haste as a brown, furry ball swept past and another not far behind. He recognized the Click's nuisance pets, which he had read were often loose on the station. These were slightly larger than a beach ball, and he could see a couple short, thin limbs as one creature grabbed a nearby pole and rushed upwards. About midway to the top the animal leapt off into the shadows and he couldn't see where it went.

A moment later the pet dropped, perhaps a fall of two floors or more, and landed a few yards from him. Before Morgan could react, the creature scrambled back to his feet and darted away, apparently no worse for the landing.

This was his first encounter with *anything* alien. He watched the pet disappear into an area off to the right, darting between two poles. A sign with glowing red letters spelling out *Market* hung between them. In a moment, the pet disappeared amid the makeshift booths.

The market had sprung up between the human and Ksa areas, both of them being trading people. The Ksa -- and the Norishi -- looked human enough that he couldn't have told one from the other at this distance and in the poor light, but he still stared.

Closer at hand on the left he found something far more familiar and somewhat comforting. The dockside work yard, with various pieces of equipment torn apart and laid out, made the odd port seem normal . . . until one of the Click pets bounded through the area. A woman with wild orange and pink hair dropped a wrench and dived at the animal, catching the creature by the fur and lifting him off the ground.

"Give it back," she said over the clinks and clanks all around them. She gave the creature a little shake. "Give it back *now*."

Limbs appeared and something square dropped into her outstretched hand. She leaned over and set the pet back on the ground, then gave the little guy the kind of friendly pat you would give to a not-so-well-trained puppy. The pet, in return, gave one slight bounce, spun and started away. The woman watched for a moment, shoved the stolen box into her pocket and unexpectedly gave three quick claps.

The pet spun and bounded back to her. Now that was *damned* interesting.

"This is for you." She pulled a wrench out of her pocket. The pet quivered with excitement as he stretched upward as she put the wrench into the creature's hands. She clapped once and the creature squeaked and flipped before he darted away.

Odd thing to give to an animal, but he could see the others at the work yard looked pleased. One slapped her on the shoulder. "Well done, Felice! Let's see if it turns up in the market!"

She smiled, noticed Morgan for the first time and gave a little nod before going back to work. He wanted to know what that had been about, but he'd wait until he had some official capacity here. They might have just told him, but he wanted people to understand he wasn't someone passing through.

As a scientist, the entire exchange intrigued him from the initial 'give it back' to the clapping which seemed to have some sort of communicative significance. He felt a chill go up his arms; a feel he always got when he found something fascinating that he didn't quite understand. That was the work he loved.

The pet had gone and the humans returned to their work, clanging on metal and using small torches to make repairs. He hadn't considered how they would have had to go back to the basics without laser-powered tools, though he did see a few with small power packs. A small tank fueled the torch and he wondered where they got the gas for it. Maybe mined it nearby. This was a rich system for gasses and minerals.

So much to learn. Most people wouldn't understand why the idea made him grin.

His eyes had begun to adjust somewhat. To the right of the market he could see the Ksa and then the Click zones, clearly marked with signs high up on the walls, and written in several languages. Ahead, he could see a signs proclaiming the human zone. To the left, beyond the work yard would be the Norishi Enclave where two guards stood, in the inevitable grey and brown outfits they all wore. Short haired, medium height -- at a distance they seemed very human. The Norishi were notoriously unfriendly, though. All but the market and the human area were red zoned to humans. Trying to cross uninvited into an alien area would get a person locked up in the makeshift detention and shipped off with the next transport, whatever it might be. The human area held the same restrictions to the aliens, but the humans tended to be more lavish with invitations.

Between the market and the entrance to the human section stood a makeshift building put together from bits of colorful plastic crates which made structure look fantastical. Light came from inside and a little laughter. The sign read *Xenobia Bar and Grill.*

Morgan headed towards the welcoming sounds. He wanted a place to sit down and take in the feel of Xenation. Besides, he knew better than to rush into the science department and upset the situation when they would only now be hearing about the changeover. Samplin wanted out, so that wouldn't be a problem, but he couldn't be certain how much Samplin had told the others. Best to let the man handle the changeover in his own way. Morgan would have time enough to strut in and flex his muscles.

However, as he reached door he heard a commotion behind him. When he looked, the wild-haired woman jogged past him and to the door. "Rafe, you here? We have problems!"

Almost immediately a tall, thin young man with long, dark hair came out the door. Morgan didn't think this could be the infamous Rafael Karim until he saw the metal plate melded to the left side of his face, a graceful curve of silver and blue that arched under his eye, across his cheek and up to the ear, disappearing into the hairline.

Morgan watched him go past thinking Rafael might be more interesting than the station itself. Rafael Karim had survived the only major disaster on Xenation and he had lived because the station saved him, grafted the metal link to his face, and sent him back to work with the others. The link supposedly kept him tied to . . . whatever ran the station. Rafe claimed not to know.

More than two hundred others had died in the accident.

Or maybe they hadn't.

Morgan hadn't expected his first look at the Displaced to happen within minutes of stepping on the station. Reports said they rarely showed themselves, but he could see the gathering of swirling white and color moving near the dark ceiling and rushing down towards the work yard.

The lights began to dim on the poles and he felt a chill -- a real chill -- in the air. Others came from Xenobia and a few from the market gathered to watch. No one looked happy.

Morgan followed Rafe to the work yard though he kept back at the line with the others who had gathered. Rafael circled the area where waves of color, mostly pale reds and oranges, began to coalesce into sinewy shapes. Morgan could see an odd reflection on the metal plate on his face -- or perhaps the surface glowed. Rafael put a hand to the surface and winced, but he shook his head and finally stepped closer to the colorful show.

The colors began to take on forms and shapes. Morgan thought they didn't look much like the traditional gauzy description of ghosts, but more like holographs with badly tuned lighting.

He looked for the projector and wondered if maybe the Click pet hadn't planted one up towards the ceiling where he couldn't see. Another of the pets had been in the work yard and could have placed a receiver there as well.

He had heard the pets were loose in the bay area, and sometimes even wandered into the Human Enclave. Having them set this up was an easy answer. Unfortunately, he also knew easy answers were rarely the real ones.

A flash of light drew his attention back to the drama before him. Rafael had his hands up, and the ghosts swarmed in moving closer to him. Not ghosts. The locals called them the Displaced. No one knew quite what the station had done (if the station really did create this illusion), but theory said they had taken those who surely would have died in the one big disaster and pulled them . . . somewhere else which might be slightly out of this reality. They did not find bodies and very little debris, but some of the science department thought everything had been disintegrated by Xenation to avoid damage.

The Displaced began to appear a few days after the disaster. Rafael's link gave him some sort of control over the apparitions -- if you believed the stories.

Others thought this a hoax. Station Master Neva NiGwen didn't believe in the Displaced or Rafael's control, and since she had been here at the time of the accident, he tended to agree with her.

This made a good show, though, and probably very entertaining for the locals who were stuck out here with very little to do but work. He watched as Rafael lifted a hand again, and wondered how he got the effect that made his hair flow out like a wind blew past him.

The lights dimmed more and the area grew decidedly colder. Then a light flashed within the swirl of colors, which had grown richer with blues, greens and lines that seemed almost black though they glowed. The light flashed again with a quick strobe of brilliant white, and Rafael took a sudden step backwards with one hand going to his chest.

"Son of a bitch," the wild-haired woman whispered. He saw her pull up her wrist and hit the commlink she wore. "Yang? This is Felice. Rafe is going to need you. We have some really annoying Displaced down at the work yards again."

The lighting grew dimmer all across the area and added a bluish caste to the scene. Rafael stood in a mass of Displaced, apparently holding them back from something while they grew more persistent. Morgan could *almost* hear words and still looked around for a projector. There had to be sign of one somewhere. Morgan also listened to the nervous whispers from the people who watched. He would have thought, living here, that they'd be used to the show by now.

"I hope he gets them in hand pretty soon," a woman said. "Otherwise we're going to be in for a long cold time before we can regain heat and power. I don't want to go through that again."

People gave general nods and grunts of agreement. Morgan didn't remember reading anything about power loss associated with these reports. Perhaps this was a recent development. It would take a lot of manipulation to drop the temp and the lighting in an area this large. He found himself intrigued by how anyone managed it.

Golden light flashed as one of the Displaced wrapped itself around a tool with a power cube. The figure brightened and others swept in, as though to suck off the power. Rafael cut between them, and reached into the mass of light as people on the dock made new sounds of worry. He yanked the power cube back away.

Morgan saw Medtech Yang arrive at a run, recognizing him both from his blue uniform and from the face in the files he'd studied. The man came to a breathless stop next to Morgan and stood there, shaking his head.

"Still at it?" he asked, looking worried.

"Still at it," Felice agreed. She ran a hand through her orange and pink hair and looked worried. "Let's hope he gets help soon."

"What happens if he loses?" Morgan asked.

"They suck down all the power they can find, ruin equipment and make life miserable," Yang replied. He frowned. "And you are?"

"Morgan Doreet, the new head of the science section."

The introduction drew quick glances of surprise and worry from some of the people, but Yang only nodded.

"Well, we'll have time to talk later," Yang said. "Right now I have to concentrate on my problem child."

Those words brought a sprinkling of laughter, though the sound hinted at worry. Morgan could see his breath now and the lights went almost dead around them as the Displaced grew brighter. He wished he had sensor equipment in hand, though he noticed Yang did. He would want to see those readings later, after the show.

"Come on, Xenation, baby," Felice whispered. She shoved her hands into her pockets, and scrunched up her shoulders, obviously cold. "We need help here."

The medtech moved closer to Rafael who waved him away. Yang didn't go closer, but he held his place, even when a couple of the displaced figures began to move his way.

"No," Rafael said quite clearly. "No, it's not him you want."

The words drew them back.

"What would happen if they decided to go to Yang instead?" Morgan asked.

"Hard to say," Felice answered. He could see goose bumps on her arms, and was glad he wore a long-sleeved shirt. "The last guy went into a coma for nearly four days. Then he left Xenation and said he'd never come back. Damn shame. He was a good tech."

So good that he might have found answers Rafe didn't want him to know? Was he chased off?

Morgan was still considering the possibility when he thought he felt a sudden change. A moment later the glowing spots in the wall nearby began to brighten and a slightly warmer breeze blew past him. He looked over his shoulder, trying to figure out where it originated.

"Finally," Felice said. "I thought Xenation had gone to sleep on us."

The faint scent of green apples grew for a moment, mingled with something less identifiable. The air warmed by several degrees which proved to be almost too much at once. Morgan felt the edge of a headache try to take him but he fought the feeling down. He didn't want anything to interfere with his perception of this entire business.

He had expected the Displaced to just disappear, but something far stranger happened. He felt little waves of wind slip past him and as each blast moved inward, something invisible seemed to grab one of the ghostly figures and drag it away from the others. The Displaced fought the movement, but they apparently had less power as individuals rather than as a whole. The lights on the poles brightened again. People began to nod and move off, looking relieved. Only Felice stayed where she was, watching Rafael and the medtech.

When almost all of the Displaced were gone, Rafael went down to his knees, his part in the show over. Morgan wanted to head into Xenobia and do some quick notes on what he had seen, as well as the incident with the Click pet leading up to it. He didn't think he would find anything particularly helpful. He didn't remember seeing anything about the pets in earlier reports about the Displaced. Had people gotten so used to seeing them that they didn't even consider their actions anymore? Not likely in a settlement made almost entirely of scientists.

He watched as the medtech got Rafael back to his feet. He looked unsteady, and in the better light, Morgan could see a line of blood running beneath the edge of the metal graft. A couple Displaced still hovered nearby and Rafael reached out towards one, as thought to call it back. Yang took hold of his arm and pulled it down, saying something too quiet for Morgan to hear. Rafael bowed his head this time and Yang had trouble holding him to his feet. Felice came to help.

Only one displaced remained, circling and drifting towards Rafael. The shape turned and started away . . . and then came to Morgan.

When the apparition stopped before him, Morgan looked into the face of an old friend: Ashur, Neva's husband. The hair stood up on the back of Morgan's neck and his heart pounded too hard. Unsettling, even the way Ashur turned his head, nodded in the old way he always had. The Displaced smiled and then began to drift away and Morgan had the urge to try and call him back, to try and understand --

No.

This could not be real. He looked to where the other two took Rafael away and reminded himself of all the reports Neva had sent him. Rafael played tricks. This was some kind of game, probably cooked up with the help of some of his alien friends; that was what Neva said. Morgan would find the real answers.

But he had looked into the face of an old friend, and Morgan suspected this was not entirely what he had been led to believe.

Thank you for purchasing my book! I hope you enjoyed the story. If you have comments or questions, please contact me.

Website: www.lazette.net
Email: Zette@lazette.net

www.ingramcontent.com/pod-product-compliance
Lightning Source LLC
Chambersburg PA
CBHW071254250626
47159CB00004B/1177